To EMI-LEI
LOTS^LOVE
TERRY x

Terry signature

Terry Tarbox worked for many years in the retail furniture trade, but has also been a postman, a milkman, an ice-cream seller and manager of a pet cemetery (a job he soon decided was not for him). Now retired, his hobbies are gardening, reading and writing. He loves working on his allotment, and that is where he thinks up most of his stories. He blames *Spike Milligan*, *The Goon Show* and *Monty Python's Flying Circus* for the level of humour in his tall tales. Having struggled with depression for many years, he cites story-writing and the strong support of his friends and family as the things which have kept him on track. He lives in Lowestoft, Suffolk.

Also by Terry Tarbox

My Mate Joe & Other Rhymes

Available from

www.willigrews.co.uk

and

Amazon

THE WILLIGREWS

Terry Tarbox

First published in England in 2011 by
The Book Guild Ltd (hardback)

Reprinted by Createspace for Amazon

Copyright © Terry Tarbox 2013

The right of Terry Tarbox to be identified as the author of this work has been asserted by him in accordance with the Copyright, Designs and Patents Act 1988

All rights reserved. No part of this publication may be reproduced, transmitted, or stored in a retrieval system, in any form or by any means, without permission in writing from the author, or be otherwise circulated in any form of binding or cover other than that in which it is published and without a similar condition being imposed on the subsequent purchaser.

All characters in this publication or fictitious and any resemblance to real people, alive or dead, is purely coincidental.

Illustrations by WW Design
ww.design@btinternet.co.uk
01825 768518

ISBN 978-1492200420

CONTENTS

The Willigrews and the Skraks   1

The Willigrews and the Time Case   23

The Willigrews and Heafod   43

The Willigrews and the Gloopudds   85

The Willigrews and the Big Sneeze   127

The Willigrews and the Half-Baked Scone   161

MAP OF WILLIGREW

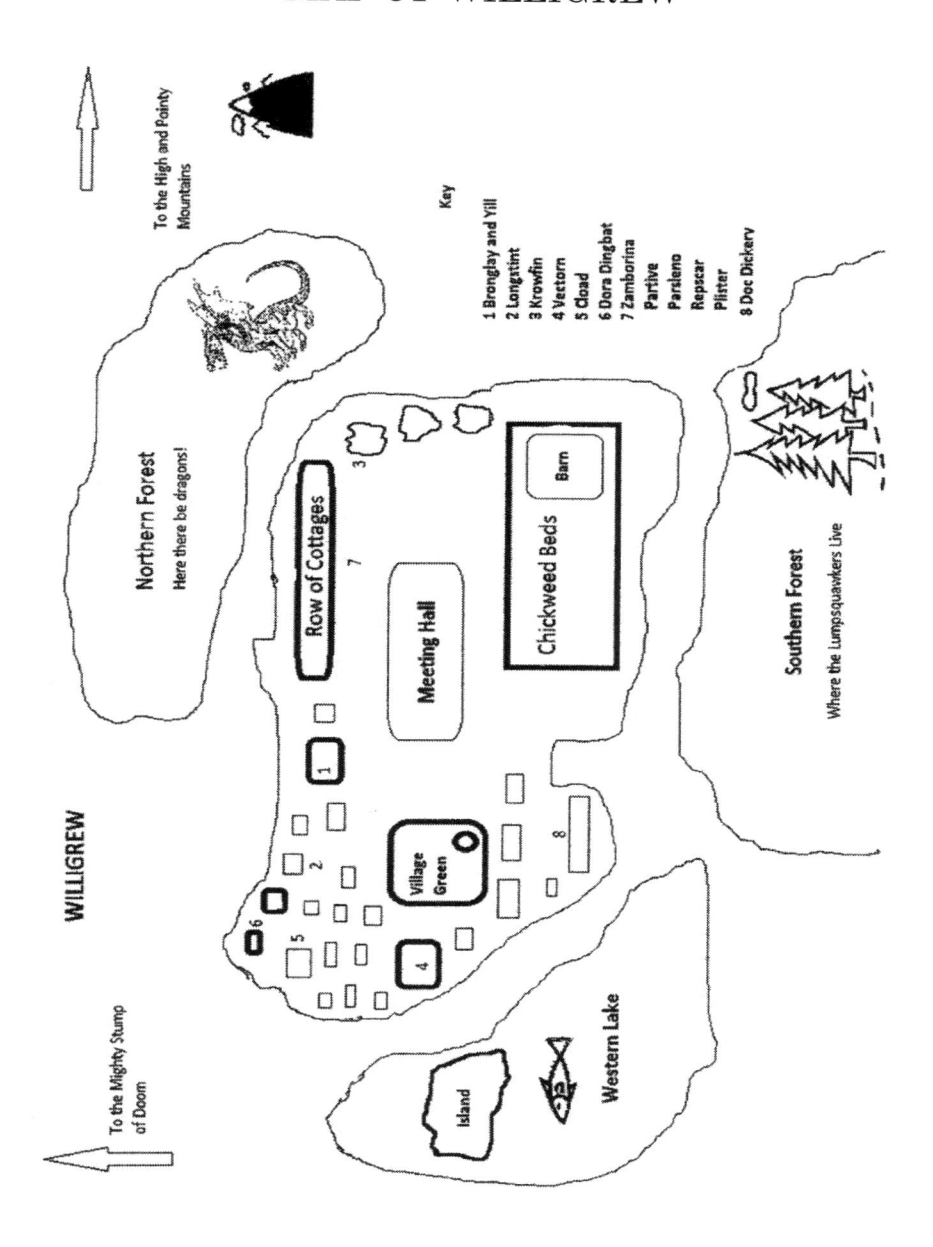

To the High and Pointy Mountains

Key

1 Bronglay and Yill
2 Longtint
3 Krowfin
4 Vectorn
5 Claad
6 Dora Dingbat
7 Zamborina
 Partive
 Parsleno
 Repscar
 Plister
8 Doc Dickery

Northern Forest
Here there be dragons!

Row of Cottages

Meeting Hall

Chickweed Beds

Barn

Southern Forest
Where the Lumpsquawkers live

WILLIGREW

Village Green

To the Mighty Stump of Doom

Island

Western Lake

THE WILLIGREWS AND THE SKRAKS

Long ago, in the distant future, in a place not far below the earth and not all that far above it, there lived a small tribe of creatures. Or should that be a tribe of small creatures? Anyway, the tribe was small and so were the creatures.

They were called the Willigrews, which was strange because not one of them was called Willie, and they never grew, which was why they were so small.

Now the Willigrews were odd-looking things. They were about the size of a golf ball (not that they ever played golf, which was just as well). They all had legs, but not all of them had the same number. It all depended on which family they came from.

Most of them, however, had two legs, which started at the bottom of their little round bodies and finished on the ground ... just.

Their arms were a sort of skinny version of their legs, except that they had hands on the end instead of feet, and stuck out from the sides of their bodies.

The Willigrews' heads were a different kettle of fish, about half the size of their bodies and a bit fatter than their arms. They had small round noses, pretty pink lips and big, big, big blue eyes (except for the ones with big, big, big brown eyes), and their bodies were covered in the brightest, silkiest, greenest fur.

The most important Willigrew was called Bronglay, which meant 'The Leader'. On becoming leader his name was changed to Bronglay, which, as it meant 'Leader', was pretty sensible. He was originally called Diamfor, which meant 'Not the Leader'.

Bronglay was chosen as leader because he had powers – magic powers. Although all the Willigrews had magic powers, only Bronglay's worked.

Bronglay was married to Yill, who was the most beautiful of all the lady Willigrews. Her fur seemed greener, and she was more graceful than the rest. Bronglay loved her very much.

They had two sons, Rewsin and Father (who was named after his father).

The Willigrews were mostly farmers. They grew chickweed, which was what they liked to eat.

Most of the time their lives were peaceful. They liked to eat and drink, they liked to sing and dance, and they lived happy, contented lives.

Other things did happen, however — otherwise this would be a pretty boring story!

The Willigrews had an enemy – a different tribe called the Skraks. The Skraks were similar to the Willigrews in size and shape, but their fur was coarser and darker in colour. They looked much spikier.

The Skraks were nasty creatures, none more so than their leader Matcher, whose favourite saying was, 'The only good Willigrew is one that isn't bad.'

Like the Willigrews, the Skraks loved chickweed, but they were a lazy lot of lumps who didn't like work, so they started stealing from the Willigrews' farms.

This meant that guards had to be posted along the border between the two states – and as the postal service wasn't much good, they always arrived late, which gave the Skraks plenty of time to steal the crops.

One dark night at the Chickweed Beds, on the border between Willigrew and Skrakland, a Willigrew named Longstint stood on guard.

He was daydreaming (yes, it was night time, but he was awake) when suddenly he was disturbed by a sound. *Munch, munch, munchy munch*, it went, followed by scuffling.

Then Longstint was amazed to hear singing.

> *Oh! Good fun, great fun!*
> *I am a Skrak.*
> *I'll eat my fill*
> *Till the Willies come back!*

Longstint was furious. Being a fully trained guard, he knew what to do. He stood on his toes and shouted, 'I know you're there, Skrak, so stop that munching!'

'I am not a Skrak,' came the reply. 'I am a blade of grass.'

Longstint gave a huff of disgust. 'You can't fool me – a blade of grass wouldn't make a munching noise!'

'It wasn't me munching, it was a small bush next to me,' said the voice. 'Small bushes are famous for making munching noises. I even heard one say "yummy" once.'

'Well,' said Longstint firmly, 'stand aside! I'm going to arrest you.'

He ran fearlessly into the darkness towards the sound, but when he got there, he found a whole group of shrubs and a squillion blades of grass.

'OK,' he said. 'Which of you bushes was munching?'

There was no answer, which annoyed the Willigrew. His nose wrinkled up, and he said, 'Well, I've got all night, so not one of you bushes is leaving until the guilty party owns up!'

Longstint sat on a small rock in front of the bushes and waited.

Of course, by now the Skrak was back across the border with a very full stomach and a carrier bag full of stolen chickweed.

Back at the Chickweed Beds, the patient Longstint was staring at the bushes. 'Sooner or later one of them will start munching or saying "yummy",' he thought. Eventually, however, he fell asleep.

When he woke in the morning, he had forgotten all about the bushes and could only remember that the weed had been stolen. He reported the theft to the guard captain and went home feeling a bit confused.

The Willigrews' leader Bronglay had tried various ways of stopping the raids. He had sent his 'right-hand man' Krowfin to speak with the Skraks' leader, Matcher, but when Krowfin returned, he was so confused he had to be made Bronglay's left-hand man.

Bronglay had even offered to supply the Skraks with free chickweed seed so they could grow their own, but the lazy lumpers were not interested.

The Willigrews were far from happy with the

way things were going. Some of them staged a protest march outside Bronglay's house.

They carried banners with slogans on them saying 'Ban the Skraks', 'Call out the Army' and 'We're far from happy with the way things are going' (see, I told you so).

These protests made Bronglay very unhappy, so he decided to act. He kept forgetting his lines, however, so instead he started making plans to solve the problem of the Skraks.

Bronglay racked his brains, but it was extremely difficult to think with a stretched-out brain, so he turned to his beloved Yill for help.

Yill smiled at her husband. 'Why don't you use your magic powers, O little green furry chap?' she said gently.

'By the pegs on a clothes line!' exclaimed Bronglay. 'Why didn't I think of that?'

He was so happy that he did a little jig, which made his fur ripple. This made Yill laugh so much that she rolled around on the floor, bumping into the furniture.

'Wait!' said Bronglay as Yill got to her feet. 'I'm in a quandary.'

'What is it?' said Yill.

'A quandary is when you don't know what to do,' he explained. 'I can only use my magic powers on Willigrews. They won't work on the Skraks.'

'But you've never actually tried,' said Yill.

'It is written,' replied Bronglay solemnly. 'That is enough for me.' There were non-believers among the Willigrews, however, who thought it was all just a story invented by the Skraks in the distant past.

Yill sat down and started to sing. She always sang when she had a problem to solve.

Down, down where the Willigrews play,
Willying and Grewing all through the day,
Little Rewsin and Great Bronglay,
All down where the Willigrews play.

I love my little warm home,
If I had a choice I'd never roam,
But I must go down to the Chickweed Bed
To keep my chubby family fed.

Down, down where the Willigrews say,
'Foam-backed carpet and underlay.'
Willigrews making pots from clay,
All down where the Willigrews play.

Having finished her song, Yill sat and thought. She thought and thought, but the only solutions she could think of were things like paint and chickweed gravy.

What could they do?

Although the Willigrews had an army, it was not the sort of army that we humans have. You see, the Willigrews were not really into violence. They were peaceful creatures and their army was used only to lift heavy things, which meant they were kept pretty busy (Willigrews being rather weak creatures, they found most things heavy).

Bronglay and Yill sat staring into space, thinking, when suddenly the door burst open and in came Krowfin, Bronglay's left-hand man. He was still confused and looked very worried.

'For highness' sake, Your Goodness!' he said. 'We must do something about the Skraks. Our tribe is very unrestless and happy!'

He stopped and frowned, but before he could correct himself Bronglay interrupted. 'I know what you mean, old friend. I understand, and I am also unhappy, but what can we do to stop them? As you know, Krowfin, my magic powers won't work on the Skraks.'

Yill spoke. 'I suppose you wouldn't consider a meeting with that nasty Matcher woman?'

'I think she's right,' said Krowfin.

Bronglay wrinkled up his nose and replied, 'I have tried many times to speak with Matcher. She doesn't listen, and you know that. She always gives me orders, and I always walk out.'

'Why not give it one more try?' said Yill. 'Things are getting pretty bad.'

After much thinking, walking up and down and standing on one leg, Bronglay decided to meet Matcher.

So between the three of them, they composed a letter which went something like this:

> Bronglay, leader of the Willigrews, would be most honoured to meet Matcher, mighty leader of the Skraks, at a neutral location of her choice, for the purpose of talking about a few things and dining on Boogaloo chickweed.

Boogaloo chickweed, let me explain, was the purest kind grown by the Willigrews and was only eaten on very special occasions.

This was sure to tempt Matcher, they thought.

The next day, at dawn, a messenger was sent with the invitation and instructions to wait for a reply. As it happened, the Boogaloo did the trick, and the messenger soon returned to Bronglay with Matcher's answer.

The whole family, plus Krowfin, were present when Bronglay read the message. It read:

> Oh, all right then, we'll meet in the Fairy Ring on the big hill tomorrow at dawn. Come alone.

News of the meeting soon spread and Bronglay received many good luck messages from his hopeful subjects. He was even interviewed by the Willigrew newspaper, *The Daily Folded Thing*, and they printed Bronglay's message to all the Willigrews. It read:

> My dear Willigrews, I can promise you, with hand on heart and arms folded, that I will do my utmost to stop this dreadful weed-nicking. If I do not return, I will see you when I do.

Next morning, as the sun began to lighten the ground around the Fairy Ring, Bronglay, having said farewell to his family, set off on his mission of peace.

As he trudged down the road, many thoughts filled his head. Would Matcher turn up? Would she be reasonable? Would it rain? What's for dinner?

When he arrived at the meeting place, it was deserted. Bronglay sat and waited. After about twenty minutes Matcher arrived.

As Matcher spent most of the time in a bad mood, and her fur was filthy and sticky, her face had become set in a permanent scowl.

She couldn't have smiled if she had wanted to. In her hand she carried a large spoon.

'Greetings, mighty Matcher,' said Bronglay, his voice a little quivery.

'Have you brought the Boogaloo?' Matcher demanded in a scratchy voice.

'A Willigrew always keeps his word,' Bronglay replied.

'He always keeps his chickweed, you mean!' snapped Matcher.

Bronglay did not want to get off on the wrong foot, so he ignored her comment and tried to start the talks.

He began by asking Matcher why the Skraks were stealing the Willigrews' crops.

'It's tradition,' she explained.

'But it only started recently,' protested Bronglay.

'Well,' Matcher said, hands on hips, 'it's a new tradition that we've just started, so there!'

'Oh dear!' cried Bronglay. 'Oooh dear, oh dear, oh dear! You really must try to be reasonable, Matcher.'

'I'll be reasonable, all right — after I've eaten that plumpety chicky weed,' replied Matcher, pointing a stiff finger towards the bag at Bronglay's feet.

BOOGALOO CHICKWEED

'I'll be reasonable, all right — after I've eaten that plumpety chicky weed,' replied Matcher, pointing a stiff finger towards the bag at

Bronglay's feet.

'OK,' said Bronglay. 'Eat your fill, but don't rush it: it's very rich.' Matcher ignored his warning, however, and Bronglay could only watch as the greedy Skrak shovelled the delicious chickweed into her mouth without even stopping, it seemed, to breathe.

'Please, Matcher,' begged Bronglay. 'Don't rush it!'

But still the Skrak munched away. *Chomp, chomp*, she went, until every last morsel had disappeared into her greedy mouth.

Bronglay squeezed his eyes tightly shut. 'You'll explode!' he shouted.

Sure enough, Matcher began to swell and her stomach began to rumble. 'Help me!' she cried. 'I'm going to pop!'

'*Water!*' screamed Bronglay in panic. 'Go to that puddle and drink some water. It's your only chance!'

'But I can't walk,' moaned Matcher.

Bronglay leapt into action. Even though he hated the very thought of touching a spiky Skrak, he wrinkled up his nose and, using only the tips of his fingers, rolled Matcher down to the puddle.

The puddle, however, was at the bottom of the hill. Half-way there Bronglay lost control and Matcher began to roll rapidly down towards the water.

'*Aaaaaagh*!' screamed the Skrak, and then there was a huge splash as she hit the water. Bronglay arrived seconds later to see Matcher thrashing around in the puddle.

'Save me!' she screamed.

Bronglay dived into the water and swam out to the helpless Skrak. He dragged her to the edge of the puddle, but before he had time to catch his breath, Matcher was shouting in a high-pitched squeaky voice, 'It's too late – I'm going to pop!'

Bronglay shook the water out of his eyes ... and stared in amazement. Matcher had changed. Gone were the dark spikes. Instead she was covered in bright green, silky fur.

'You're a Willigrew!' gasped Bronglay. 'The water has washed you clean.'

Skraks, he realised, must be lazy Willigrews who never washed. He had always thought they seemed a bit smelly.

'You're a Willigrew,' he repeated.

But Matcher was not listening. She was desperately clutching her stomach, which was now twice its normal size. 'Oooooh pop!' she squeaked. 'Pop, pop, pop! I'm done for!'

Bronglay was still recovering from the shock of having seen a Skrak turn into a Willigrew when suddenly a thought entered his befuddled brain.

'Magic, magicky, magic!' he thought. 'If Matcher is a Willigrew, I can use my magic.'

It was a while since Bronglay had used his magic powers, but he knew that he had to cast a spell in rhyme, and he had to do it quickly as Matcher was about to explode.

'*Think*!' he told himself.

Gathering his thoughts, he said, 'Right, here goes.'

Ploppety plop, wippety wop,
Don't let old Matcher go poppety pop.
And if she's OK at the end of the day,
Make her behave in a reasonable way.

Bronglay stood and looked at Matcher's tum, hoping against hope that it would not explode.

At last her stomach began to shrink. It happened slowly at first, but sure enough, within a few minutes, after much fuss and groaning from her, it was back to normal.

The little Skrak stood up and felt her stomach. She looked at Bronglay and, to his surprise, she smiled and said, 'Bronglay, little fluffy Brongers! My dear, dear old friendy, my little Brongaloony! You have saved my life, and now I am a fluffsome Willigrew, just like you.'

She ran to Bronglay and hugged him, and then the two little creatures danced a jig in the bright morning sunshine.

When they were quite exhausted, they linked arms and went off to tell everyone what had happened.

As soon as Matcher arrived home, she passed a law ordering all Skraks to wash in the big puddle, so they all became Willigrews.

Yill organised a big party, and she invited all the old Willigrews and all the new Willigrews.

At the party it was decided that Matcher and Bronglay would take it in turns to rule the Willigrews. It was also decided that Matcher's name, which meant 'Spiky and Unreasonable', would be changed to Vectorn, which meant 'One Whose Stomach Nearly Exploded by the Puddle and Who Was Now Pretty Nice'.

At the end of the party Krowfin announced that he would entertain everyone with a song about the new peace – but, confused as ever, he did a conjuring trick instead and pulled a hat out of a rabbit.

Everybody laughed and went home happy.

To Bronglay's delight, everything from that day onwards quietened down. All the Willigrews returned to a peaceful, happy life, until one day…

But that is another story, so do read on.

THE WILLIGREWS AND THE TIME CASE

Now, the Willigrews spent most of their lives feeling a bit confused, and I think I should explain why.

You see, it had something to do with the way their bodies were designed.

A typical Willigrew had all the normal bits and pieces, nose, eyes, feet, knees, mouth, and so on, but unlike us humans, theirs were all positioned on the backs of their bodies. That meant that all the things that should have been behind them were in front — things like shoulder blades, heels, bottoms and spines.

To get around this problem, the Willigrews decided long ago that in order to avoid bumping into things, not to mention each other (sorry I said I wouldn't mention each other, whoops, I mentioned it again!), they would have to spend their whole lives walking backwards.

This, I hope, will explain why they were a touch confused. It doesn't explain why I am confused, but there you are. I think. Well, you must be there otherwise you wouldn't be reading this, would you?

Without a doubt, the most confused Willigrew was Krowfin. He was Bronglay's left-hand man.

He was even seen on some occasions walking forwards, which meant he often had to visit Doc Dickory (who was named after his great-grandmother's favourite nursery rhyme) to have various bumps and bruises treated.

Krowfin had no lady Willigrew as a partner, and he lived alone amongst the roots of a tall oak tree, his front door being just above the ground.

Krowfin's favourite pastime was sitting in his favourite chair with his feet on his second favourite stool and counting his blessings.

He thought, for example, of how lucky he was

not to have caught a cold three weeks ago when Doc Dickory was on holiday.

Then he thought how lucky he was not to have been hit by a falling tree branch, and how fortunate it was that the branch hadn't fallen in the first place.

On one particular night, as Krowfin sat counting his blessings, he heard a noise coming from outside. It was very late and all the other Willigrews should have been in bed. He decided to take a look. He opened his front door and peered into the darkness. He looked left and right, but saw nothing.

'Must have been my imagination, although that never made a noise before,' he thought. He turned to go back inside, but as he did so, he heard the sound again. He listened intently and this time he heard a voice – a small quivery voice.

'Can you tell me where I am, without hitting me?' the voice said.

Then Krowfin saw the creature that had spoken. It was about half his size with a skinny little orange body, completely hairless, and it had a long face with its eyes, nose and mouth all scrunched into the bottom half. It looked very frightened.

'Please, mighty one, please tell me where I am and don't bash me. I don't like being bashed,' the creature pleaded.

Krowfin said, feeling a bit annoyed, 'I am a Willigrew, and we don't bash anybody. You had better come in out of the cold and tell me who you are.' (He really meant '*what* you are', but didn't want to sound rude.)

The unfortunate creature sat down by the fire and Krowfin made him a cup of chickweed tea.

'Now then, little chap, who are you and where do you come from?' Krowfin asked.

'I'm called Cringe and I come from Wimp,' the creature told him. 'I was playing with my dad's Time Case when there was a flash, and I ended up here, wherever here is.'

'But where is Wimp?' asked Krowfin. 'I've never heard of it.'

'Wimp is here,' said Cringe, 'but in a different time. You see, the Time Case allows my dad to travel across time. It's a special power he has, and it seems I have it too.'

'That's unbelievable!' gasped Krowfin.

'I don't want to disagree with you, Your Sirness, in case you give me a sound thrashing, but I'm afraid it's true,' said Cringe … cringing.

'Look,' said Krowfin impatiently, screwing up his nose and throwing it in the bin. 'Willigrews don't believe in all that sound thrashing stuff.'

Cringe went on to explain that his name meant 'One Who Is Frightened of His Own Shadow Even When He Isn't Casting One'. He then looked up at Krowfin with tearful eyes and pleaded, 'Please help me, Your Largeness. I'm lost and very, very frightened.' He then began crying and weeping and sobbing. The tears poured down his skinny orange face.

'Now, now,' said Krowfin. 'Don't take on so, you're safe here with me. You get a good night's sleep and in the morning I'll take you to our leader. He will know what to do.'

The little creature fell fast asleep where he sat. Krowfin looked down at little Cringe and smiled. 'No one will bash you in Willigrew,' he said quietly, then he too curled up in front of the fire and fell asleep.

In the morning Krowfin woke Cringe, and after drinking some tea they set off to see Bronglay.

When they arrived at the leader's home, Bronglay, Yill and their two sons Rewsin and Father were eating breakfast. When Krowfin entered the room with Cringe holding his hand tightly, the whole family turned and gasped with surprise.

'*What* on earth is *that?*' asked Rewsin, not being as choosy with his words as Krowfin had been.

Krowfin explained the situation as clearly as he could, considering it was morning, which was when he was at his most confused.

Yill took pity on Cringe and, sitting next to him, said, 'Don't you worry, my little satsuma. Bronglay will find a way to get you back to Wimp before you can say your name.'

Cringe said, 'Your name,' and waited, but nothing happened.

This made everybody laugh and they all did a hopping dance around the room until Krowfin bumped into a cupboard, having forgotten to hop backwards. Then they all sat down to think of a way to help Cringe. All, that is, except Krowfin, who knelt on a chair and faced the wrong way.

As they sat and knelt and pondered, Yill sang a little song in a soft voice.

> *It's a lovely time in the Chickweed Beds*
> *When harvest time is here,*
> *When the children dance the whole day long*
> *And we all drink chickweed beer*
> *(That beer, and we all drink chickyweed beer).*

When we all go to the clearing
And dance our hops and jigs,
Where the fiddler plays his fiddle
To the sound of breaking twigs
(Those twigs, to the sound of breaking twigs).

Ah! It's good to be a Willigrew
With a song on all our lips,
Except, that is, for Krowfin,
For when everybody hops, he hips
(He hips, for when everybody hops, he hips).

Now Cringe is such a little chap
With his wrists all skinny and limp,
But I know that we will get him back
To his Mum and Dad in Wimp
(In Wimp, to his Mum and Dad in Wimp).

All the Willigrews applauded Yill's song, while Cringe just scratched his head.

'Right,' said Bronglay. 'Any suggestions?'

'Well,' said Krowfin, 'I don't see how we can send someone across time. I mean, where would we start?'

'We can't give up that easily,' said Yill.

The rest agreed.

'I suppose we could try to make one of those Time Case things if Cringe could describe it,' suggested Rewsin.

'Do you think you could, Cringe?' Bronglay asked.

'I'll try,' Cringe replied.

'It's sort of round,' he began, 'with glass on one side and metal on the other, and underneath the glass there are numbers all around the edge. In the centre is a screw with two metal sticks attached and these point to the numbers.'

'Wait a minute!' exclaimed Yill. 'That sounds like a clock. But how can a clock transport someone across time?'

Cringe answered, 'Many sorries, Your

Kindliness, but in Wimp we call it a Time Case, and my father uses special magic words to make it work.'

'But if it's an ordinary clock that needs your father's magic words,' asked Bronglay, 'how did *you* make it work?'

'I must have stumbled across the right words,' replied Cringe.

'That would explain part of some of it,' said Krowfin, stumbling into the conversation himself, and becoming more confused by the minute.

Bronglay knelt down in front of the little orange creature and explained that if he could remember what he had said, the problem would be solved and he could be home in a flash.

At Bronglay's request, Father brought a clock from the kitchen and gave it to Cringe.

'Now you sit there and try to remember what you said,' said Bronglay.

'Take your time, my little kumquat,' added Yill, who had taken a shine to the unfortunate Cringe.

Cringe sat and stared into space, muttering things that he might have said. 'What time is dinner, Mum?' 'When will Dad be home?' 'Is that a knock at the door?' 'I hope nobody decides to bash me today.' 'Is this Time Case slow?'

Then suddenly, to everyone's surprise and delight, Cringe disappeared in a flash of orange light.

He did it!' shouted Father. 'He did it!'

But even as they were congratulating each other, there was another orange flash and, when it had cleared, there in the chair, dripping wet, sat little Cringe, his bottom lip quivering.

'Whatever happened?' Yill asked.

'I d-don't know,' answered Cringe. 'B-but I went somewhere, and it was very d-dark and wet, and it certainly w-wasn't W-wimp.' Then he began to cry.

Krowfin put an arm around Cringe – it was Yill's arm – and said, 'I'll get a bath from the towel room … I mean, I'll get a room from the bath towel…' He stamped his foot in frustration. 'Oh! I'll get something to dry him with…' and he dashed out of the room.

'So, back to square one,' sighed Krowfin a minute later as he dabbed Cringe's face with the towel.

'Not quite,' argued Bronglay. 'At least we know roughly what he has to say to make the clock work, if not how to steer it. We will just have to try again.'

'That could be pretty dangerous,' warned Yill.

'Well, it's either that or he stays here for ever,' said Bronglay.

With that Cringe began to cry again. So did Krowfin.

'Don't cry,' said Bronglay. 'We'll think of something. I know, try to say the same words in a different order.'

'What do you mean?' asked Cringe, sniffing.

'Say, "This Time Case is slow",' instructed Bronglay.

Cringe did so. There were another two flashes, one when he went and another when he came back.

'Missed again,' said Cringe dejectedly. This time he was covered in some sort of sticky mud.

'You'd better have a bath before you try again,' suggested Yill.

But just as she began to lead Cringe to the bathroom, there was another huge flash and when the smoke cleared ... there in the room stood a huge ... *thing*.

'Yerks!' whispered Krowfin. 'What is it?'

Before them stood a large brown monster with sticky mud all over its body. Its skin was leathery and glistening, its eyes were blood red and wobbled around loosely in deep sockets, and little bubbles came from its shapeless mouth.

'GRAAARK!' it shouted, making everyone jump with fright.

It stared at the little group, who had huddled together around Bronglay.

Then, from somewhere within its wet, squirming body came the words, 'Where the Dickens am I, and who are you lot?'

'I beg your pardon,' said Bronglay, trying to sound confident, which he most certainly wasn't.

'Well,' said the monster, 'I was sitting quietly in my swamp, pressing some flowers, and *poof!* I was suddenly here.'

The Willigrews stared.

'GRAAARK!' roared the monster again.

'Graaark, indeed,' said Krowfin politely. 'That's the sort of experience that would make anyone say "graaark". I would feel a bit graaarkish myself if that happened. Eh? Old friend, old pal, old slimy chap...'

Everyone looked at Krowfin, so he stopped mumbling and scratched his head.

'It's m-my fault,' admitted Cringe, nervously. 'S-so if you're going to p-punch me, g-get it over with quickly.'

'Punch you?' said the monster. 'I've a good mind to eat you, only I'm a vegetarian. You're not a vegetable by any chance, are you? Only you put me in mind of a carrot I once ate ... You see, I'm a bit peckish.'

Yill passed the monster a bowl of chickweed which it pushed, bowl included, into its slobbery mouth.

'Thanks a lot,' it said. 'That was really tasty, you must give me the recipe.'

Bronglay assured the monster that none of them were vegetables and asked what its name was.

'I am called Elbroff, which means "Someone Who Gives People Bad Headaches by Shouting Graaark a Lot",' it said.

Bronglay welcomed Elbroff to Willigrew and then said, 'Now, how are we going to get you two back to your own times? What shall we do? I haven't a clue.'

No sooner had Bronglay spoken that Elbroff disappeared in a large flash. This time, much to everybody's relief, there was no second flash.

'That's it!' shouted Yill excitedly. 'You said a rhyme and your magic worked! That's the answer.'

'Yes!' Krowfin agreed. 'All you've got to do is think of a rhyme to send little Cringe home to

Wimp.'

'Right,' said Bronglay. 'I must concentrate.' Then he walked up and down the room while Krowfin walked down and up.

'Dah, de-dah de-dah de-dah...' muttered Bronglay as he walked, trying to get it right. He tried to think of a rhyme that would send Cringe home to stay and prevent anyone or anything coming back.

Krowfin also tried to make some suggestions for a suitable rhyme. 'What about this little beauty?' he asked. 'Chickweed is green and it isn't blue, eat some now and everything will be all right in the morning.'

'You big dollop!' said Rewsin, rolling his eyes.

'Thank you,' said Krowfin, rolling them back.

By now Cringe had had a bath and his orange skin was gleaming as he came into the room. 'Have you thought of anything yet, Bronglay?' he asked, feeling a bit more confident now that he realised nobody would bash him.

'I think I have,' answered Bronglay. 'So I should say your goodbyes, because if it works you will never see us again.'

Cringe thanked everybody for not hitting him or prodding him with sharp sticks, kissed Yill and then sat and waited for Bronglay to begin his spell:

Make this work like it did with the Skrak.
Send our friend off, but send nothing back.
Wimp is a nice place as everybody knows.
This is little Cringe, and off he goes.

The spell worked immediately, with the usual flash of orange light as Cringe disappeared. The Willigrews waited for a few minutes, but nothing else happened.

'I'll miss little Cringe,' said Yill, breaking the silence (which she swept up later).

They all agreed.

'I suppose I can go home now it's all over,' said Krowfin, and he headed for the door.

But he stopped when Yill said, 'One thing is bothering me: how do we *know* Cringe is safely back in Wimp?'

Bronglay put his hand on her shoulder and said, 'I guess we'll never know, my little furry love, but I like to think he is.'

After everyone had left, Yill sat humming a sad little tune and stared at the chair where Cringe had sat. As she stared, she saw a tiny little flash of orange light just above her head.

When it faded, a small piece of orange paper drifted down and settled on her lap.

She picked it up and read the words: 'Thank you. I did get home to Wimp!'

THE WILLIGREWS AND HEAFOD

It was a normal happy day in Willigrew. At the Chickweed Beds a small group sowed seeds while others weeded among the plants.

Krowfin the Confused (as he was now known) was having a rest, sitting against a rock drinking a cup of chickweed tea. Next to him sat Rewsin.

They had been sitting quietly for a time when Krowfin turned to Rewsin and asked him a question – a question that would bring about the most exciting adventure the Willigrews had ever had.

'Who do you think was the first Willigrew?'

'I haven't a clue,' answered Rewsin. 'Do you know?'

'No,' Krowfin replied, 'that's why I asked!'

They decided that they would really like to find out and that their leader Bronglay was bound to know. Later that day, when they had finished work, they went to see Bronglay, who was helping his wife Yill to prepare dinner.

'Hello, you two,' he said as they entered. 'Would you like to stay for dinner, Krowfin old chap? There's plenty to go round.'

'No, thanks all the same,' replied Krowfin. 'I don't like my food going round. It makes me dizzy.'

Bronglay chuckled and told Krowfin he would keep his plate still. Krowfin thanked him and took his place at the table with the others, who had now been joined by Father, Bronglay's other son.

Before they ate, they observed the Willigrew tradition of sticking their fingers in their ears and singing together, 'Thanks for the chickyweed, get stuck in.'

When they had eaten, Krowfin turned to Bronglay and said, 'We've got a question for you, haven't we, Rewsin?'

Rewsin nodded.

Krowfin continued, 'We were wondering if you knew who the very first Willigrew was, and if you could tell us about him?'

Bronglay sat thinking for a time.

Yill said, 'Ten past three.'

Having got the time, he stopped thinking and said, 'Do you know, I haven't the slightest idea. I have never heard anyone tell a story about the first Willigrew.'

They all agreed that they would like to find out, so they put a poster up on the noticeboard outside the Meeting Hall, where all the Willigrews met on the third Saturday in the fourth week of every quarter in any month that did not have a W in it. The poster read:

> To all Willigrews
> Would anyone who knows anything about the very first Willigrew please contact Bronglay as soon as possible or, if possible, sooner.

As Willigrew was not a big place, news soon spread about the notice.

> **To All Willigrews**
>
> Would anyone who knows anything about the very first Willigrew please contact Bronglay as soon as possible......
>
> or if possible
> .... sooner.
>
> Bronglay

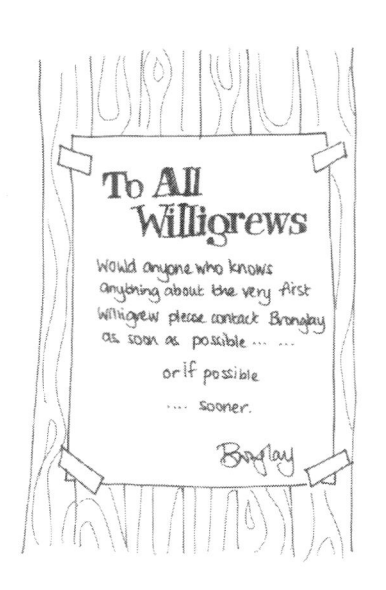

It was not long before a queue formed outside Bronglay's house.

Bronglay saw them one at a time and Yill made them each a drink.

The first Willigrew to see Bronglay was called Strif. He told his leader that he remembered his grandfather telling him a story about a very old Willigrew called Clodger who had to out-think a brain that had escaped through someone's ear and was frightening everybody.

Bronglay also remembered that story and said, 'Good thought, Strif, but in the story there was mention of Clodger's father, so he couldn't have been the first.'

Bronglay thanked Strif and the little

Willigrew left.

Next to enter was a very, very old wise man of the tribe called Cload, whose bones creaked as he moved.

He sat, and after getting his breath back, he spoke. 'I don't think you will find a single Willigrew who knows how our tribe started, but there is a strange thought in the furthest corner of my old memory that is telling me something.

Yes, that's it,' he said. 'Deep below the earth, in a giant cavern, lives a creature with a small body and a gigantic head. It once lived on the surface, but every time it learned something new its head grew a bit, and eventually it started to sink into the ground. You see, the more it knows the deeper it goes.

Its name is Heafod, and it would certainly know.'

Bronglay replied, 'Well, that's a marvellous idea, old wise man, but if he lives so far underground, how on earth are we going to find him?'

'Not *on earth*,' said Cload with a chuckle. '*Under earth*, you mean! You must first find the home of the Red Badger, who lives in the forest north of here, then if you can pass a test, he will let you into the tunnel that leads to Heafod's cavern.'

'I will have to hold a meeting to see if we really want to find this Heafod,' Bronglay told Cload. He thanked him and asked Yill to tell the Willigrews still waiting outside that they could go home.

Later that week a meeting was held at the Meeting Hall. The whole tribe attended the meeting and, after much debating and discussing, it was decided that the majority wanted to find out about the first Willigrew and that Bronglay plus two male and two female Willigrews should go.

The two male Willigrews were Krowfin and

Longstint (who was in the army). The two females were Zamborina, who was a history teacher, and Dora Dingbat, who had no special skills but was fun to have around and would keep the party cheerful.

The party met outside the Meeting Hall at daybreak the next day. Zamborina looked very intelligent and thoughtful as usual. She always carried a book, *The History of the Willigrews*, around with her and loved to talk about the past.

She considered spectacles too modern, so wore a monocle in each eye. However, her eyes were blue, her lips were pink and she was just as beautiful as all the others in her tribe.

Dora, on the other hand, always looked happy and 'up for a laugh'.

She had three little curls on top of her head, a beauty spot on her left cheek and a tiny pair of spectacles balanced on her little button nose.

She always wore cherries (fresh every day) for earrings, just in case she felt a bit peckish at any time.

Krowfin was about five minutes late because when he left his home, confused as usual, he walked forwards, which to the Willigrews was the wrong way, so he ended up further away than when he started out.

Bronglay greeted everyone. 'Well, here we all are,' he said.

'And off we all go,' said Krowfin, chuckling quietly. He gave a little hiccup and scratched his head when he bumped into the Meeting Hall door.

'Wait a minute,' said Bronglay. 'I want to say a few words.'

Everyone fell silent.

Bronglay stood proudly before the group and

said, 'A few words.'

With that, the little band of adventurers set off towards the forest to the north.

As they walked, Dora Dingbat entertained them with a really silly song, which went something like this:

> *Quitchy pitchy poo*
> *Waggle gaggle noo*
> *Niggly noggly maydee*
> *Eat your chickweed daily.*
>
> *Wonky nonky woile*
> *Dinky plinky stoile*
> *Stibby stobby stubby*
> *It will keep you chubby.*

Then the rest joined in with the chorus.

> *Niggly womp, diggly flap*
> *All day long*
> *Whimmley wo, snobbly bum*
> *Can't go wrong.*

Then they all hopped backwards, flicking their earlobes, which was the Willigrew national dance.

They all stopped dancing, however, when up ahead, blocking the pathway, they saw a crowd of creatures.

The Willigrews approached carefully, not knowing what to expect (and how could they, as I haven't even decided what's going to happen yet!).

The crowd up ahead consisted of beings that were about the same size as the Willigrews, but completely hairless. Bronglay could tell they were in an ugly mood: they were carrying banners saying 'I feel like a bent nose' and 'I feel like a cauliflower ear' and 'I feel like a big lump with hairs sticking out of it'.

As the Willigrews neared the mob, one of

them stepped forward and held up his hand (with his other hand). 'You can't come through here, brother, this is an official picket line,' he said gruffly.

'Well,' said Bronglay, 'we would never dream of crossing an official picket line. We are Willigrews and we never do what you think we wouldn't do, or what you think we would do except when we don't ... but why are you on strike?'

'You see,' explained the creature, 'it's like this 'ere. We are the Brothers and I am Frater, the Shop Steward. We exist to put things right for the underprivileged and put-upon workers of the world, workers who've been sold down the river and left all at sea and up the creek without a paddle, like.'

'Ah!' said Bronglay. 'And who are you supporting this time?'

'Well,' Frater replied, shrugging his hairless shoulders, 'nobody at this precise moment, cos there's nothing 'appening, but we're just practising, so as soon as we *are* needed, we'll be ready, like. Oh yes,' he continued, 'as soon as an offer's on the table and our brothers don't like it, we'll be away!'

'But we have no intention of breaking a strike or anything,' said Bronglay politely.

'You sure?' asked Frater. 'You sure you're not a bunch of blacklegs?'

'Certainly not!' said Bronglay, bristling with indignation. 'As you can see, we Willigrews all have *green* legs.'

'Well, I suppose we could let you pass,' said Frater grudgingly. 'But only if you donate something to our Union funds.'

At this point Krowfin shouted, 'Willigrews eat chickweed, not doughnuts!'

Ignoring this remark, Bronglay took a bag from his pocket and offered it to Frater.

'What's in 'ere then?' Frater asked.

'Nothing,' said Bronglay.

'Nothing?' exclaimed Frater. 'Wodya mean, *nothing*?'

'Well,' explained Bronglay, 'one day, when you're standing around with nothing to do, just open the bag and you'll find some nothing to do it with. It's a lot better than something, you know – you can find something any day of the week, something can be found anywhere, but just you try looking around for nothing, you'll have a job.'

'Thanks,' said Frater, 'but I've already got a job. This bag of nothing will come in 'andy, though. Where did you buy it?'

'In a shop,' answered Bronglay. 'It's just down the road, it should still be open.'

'An open shop?' gasped Frater. 'We can't 'ave that! We only allow closed shops! We're off...'

Frater and his followers rushed off in the direction Bronglay had indicated, leaving the Willigrews to continue their journey, which they did, after praising their leader for being so clever and getting the Brothers to move out of their way.

However, Bronglay had just told a lie to get his friends past the picket line, so, as was the tradition among Willigrews, he had to recite a little rhyme:

Dibby dib dib,
I told a fib,
But it was for the best,
So let my conscience rest.

Then the others joined in:

*Dobby dob, dob,
We all heard it,
But it didn't bring harm,
So it won't cause alarm.*

When night fell, the little band was under a tree so it didn't hit any of them. They made camp there, lit a fire, brewed some tea and then sat in a little circle.

Zamborina spoke first. 'Weren't we lucky to find this little circle to sit in?' she said.

But before anyone could reply, a voice which came from behind some bushes repeated exactly what Zamborina had just said.

'What was that?' said Longstint.

'What was that?' said the voice.

'It's an echo,' said Krowfin, as the body to which the voice belonged came out of the bushes and walked over to the group.

'That's right,' the creature said. 'Ann Echo, that's what everyone calls me, calls me, calls me.'

'But you're a Willigrew!' said Bronglay, because she certainly looked like one.

'No, I don't only copy voices. I copy bodies as well. It's really good fun.'

'But what do you really look like?' asked Dora.

'I can't remember,' said Ann. 'It's so long since I was myself.'

'Well, I'll be blowed!' exclaimed Krowfin. 'An echo – and I thought that an echo was a repetition of sound produced by sound waves reflected from an object denser than the aerial medium. It just goes to show you.'

'You can say that again,' said Dora, and Ann Echo did, much to everyone's amusement.

'While you're here,' said Bronglay, 'would you like something to eat?'

'No thanks,' replied Ann, 'I don't like food, it repeats on me.'

Everyone laughed again.

'I'll be on my way now,' said Ann (several times). 'I'm so glad we met, met, met.'

The Willigrews waved goodbye and Ann Echo disappeared back into the forest. After she had gone, the little band settled down for the night.

Early next morning, Bronglay was the first to rise, but soon came back down when he hit his head on a tree branch.

'Wake up, you lot!' he said softly. They all had some breakfast and started out again, trudging along the woodland path.

'I trust everyone slept well?' asked Zamborina.

'I don't know,' said Dora, 'I was asleep at the time.'

It was another three days before the Willigrews saw even a hint of what they were searching for. They found a large sign which read:

THIS WAY TO THE BADGER'S SECRET SET

Beneath these words was an arrow pointing towards a narrow path.

'I reckon that could be a clue,' said Krowfin.

'Not much gets past you,' replied Bronglay.

They followed the path for about an hour, and then they came upon a smaller sign which said:

NEARLY THERE

After a further half an hour, the path widened into a small clearing. In one corner was a large hole with yet another sign above it, showing an arrow pointing down and the words:

THIS IS IT FOLKS
THE RED BADGER'S SECRET SET
BUT DON'T TELL ANYONE

Everybody ready?' asked Bronglay. They all nodded, so in they went.

Inside it was very dark and damp, but they

soon came to a wide cavern, which was lit by a group of glow-worms. Sitting in the corner behind a desk was the badger.

'Oh! Isn't he beautiful!' gasped Dora, as she gazed at the creature who was, indeed, covered completely in bright red fur.

The badger heard this, smiled and said, 'Thank you, you too are beautiful, as are all your friends, in fact, everything and everyone is beautiful today. I'm in such a happy, dillybumptious mood!'

'Dilly what?' asked Longstint.

'Dillybumptious,' said the badger. 'Some days I feel wogglynimphous, some days I feel nogglybamptious, but today I feel dillybumptious. My name is Red Badger,' he continued, 'but my friends call me Red Badger for short. So, how can I help you?'

Bronglay replied, 'We were wondering if it would be possible to meet Heafod.'

'HEAFOD?' roared Red Badger, the sound shaking the cavern wall. 'You want to see *Heafod*? Did you say *Heafod*?'

'Er, yes,' said Bronglay, timidly.

'Oh! I thought that's what you said,' said Red Badger, smiling suddenly. 'Why, certainly, dear boy, but first you must pass a test.'

'Okey-dokey,' said Krowfin, prancing on the spot like a boxer getting ready to fight. 'We're ready. Fire away! Lay it on us, baby! We can handle tests, we're Willigrews!'

Everyone stared at Krowfin, who stood still suddenly and dropped his eyes in embarrassment. After picking them up and putting them back in, he apologised.

'Now,' said Red Badger, moving on hastily. 'On that wall, behind the curtain, is a question – yes, just one question. If you can answer it, you may enter. Be warned, however, the journey to Heafod's cave is a perilous one and it is possible that some – or even all – of you may never return.'

'We're ready,' said Bronglay bravely.

Longstint stood to attention, saluted and said, 'We're with you, leader, to the death!'

'Righty ho,' the badger said, drawing the curtain back to reveal the question. 'But think carefully before answering, as I can only accept your first answer. So this is your starter for 10 and no conferring, 10 points, I said, that's all you need, 10 points ... and what do points make?'

'Prizes!' they all answered together, not really knowing why.

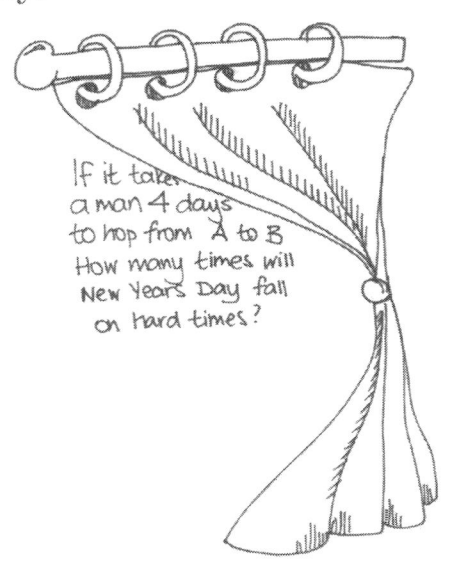

High on the wall, written in large letters, was the question:

IF IT TAKES A MAN FOUR DAYS TO HOP FROM A TO B, HOW MANY TIMES WILL NEW YEAR'S DAY FALL ON HARD TIMES?

'Why,' laughed Dora, 'that's just nonsense – silly, soppy, dopey! We'll never answer that!'

'The answer is very sensible,' said the badger. 'So think about it, and remember you still have all your lifelines, you're just one question away from a million.'

The Willigrews looked puzzled, and went to stand in a little huddle in the corner. The huddle was just big enough for five. Red Badger explained that he had picked it up cheap in the antiques department at the local Huddles-Are-Us store.

Alas, hard as they tried, the Willigrews could not think of an answer to such a silly question. They were thinking of giving up and going home, when Bronglay remembered that Red Badger had said the answer was *sensible*. They all agreed that giving a sensible answer was worth a try.

They all came out of the huddle, and

Zamborina closed the door behind her.

Bronglay looked Red Badger in the eye and said, 'The answer is: *Always brush your teeth before going to bed.*'

Everything went quiet.

Red Badger broke the silence (but explained it was an old silence, so it didn't matter) by asking, 'Confident? Final answer?'

The Willigrews nodded.

'Correct, correct, *correctamundo*! That is the right answer!' shouted Red Badger.

All the Willigrews hopped about shouting 'Whoopee-doopee!' and so on.

'But wait,' said Red Badger, holding up a paw. 'You have a choice of prizes. You can have free entry into the tunnel, or an expensive, state-of-the-art, 150-centimetre widescreen television and DVD player. Yes, you can record all your favourite programmes in the comfort of your own homes!'

The Willigrews had never heard of televisions or DVD players, so they decided they would settle for free entry into the tunnel.

'Then it only remains for me to wish you all the very best of luck.' Having said that, Red Badger opened a door and the Willigrews went into the dark tunnel beyond.

Red Badger had given them each a glow-worm to light the way, so they marched forward through the tunnel, not saying anything, until Dora complained that her glow-worm had gone out.

It soon came back in, though, so they continued until Bronglay shouted 'Stop!' and pointed to a large shadow on the wall up ahead.

'Cripes, what is it?' gulped Dora.

She did not have to wait long to find out, for just then a huge, hairy spider scuttled round the corner, growling and snarling.

'GOTCHA!' it screamed. 'You're all doomed! I'm going to wrap you all up in some silky webby stuff and suck your innards out!'

Its hairy legs bristled as the Willigrews drew back in fear. All except Longstint, that is, who stood his ground.

Looking the spider straight in the eye (it only had one), he said loudly, 'Wait a minute, you big hairy whelk, spiders can't talk. Everybody knows that!'

The spider grinned sheepishly. 'Can't they?' he asked. 'Well, in that case I suppose I'm not a spider ... how embarrassing...' He shuffled his feet as he looked at Longstint. 'They do growl a bit, though, don't they?'

'Oh yes,' Longstint agreed. 'In my experience, they growl quite a lot – but they never talk, so be on your way and let us through.'

With that the big spider skulked off round the corner, muttering to himself, 'I wonder what I am then? A pigeon? Perhaps I'm a pigeon...'

'Pigeons don't talk either!' shouted Longstint after him. 'They just go *coo*!'

'Oh, all right,' said the spider crossly. 'Don't keep on. I'm going.' But as he disappeared into the dark tunnel, the Willigrews could hear him saying, 'Coo, coo ... I *could* be a pigeon. Blooming know-all...'

The others praised Longstint for being so brave and clever, and the journey continued.

After much turning left, turning right, going straight on, doubling back, doubling forward and standing still looking confused, the Willigrews came to an entrance, above which was a sign saying:

TO HEAFOD'S CAVE.
IF YOU WISH TO ENTER, BE WARNED:
THE ROAD TO THE TRUTH IS
FILLED WITH GREAT DANGER.
ONLY THE PURE IN HEART,
STRONG IN MIND, SOUND IN BODY,
AND THOSE WEARING CLEAN SOCKS
MAY ENTER.
PLEASE MIND THE STEP.

'Sounds very nasty to me,' said Dora Dingbat, hopping nervously from one foot to the other.

'Don't worry, I'll mind the step,' said Bronglay, as he led his little group through the entrance. They had only taken a few steps when they came upon another entrance and yet another sign, which read:

ARE YOU SURE NOW?

On went the little fivesome, through the entrance and onwards. Nothing much seemed to be happening. Zamborina was just about to say, 'So far, so good,' when Longstint shouted out in pain.

'*Aaaaagh!*' he yelled. 'Get it off me!'

Bronglay spun around. To his horror, he saw that Longstint was being dragged away by a large earlug (an earlug, let me explain, is like an earwig, but it has its own hair).

Longstint was clasped firmly in the earlug's pincers. He struggled and wriggled and fought bravely, but although he was in the army and stronger than most Willigrews, he was no match for the mighty earlug.

The others gave chase as the insect scuttled off with their little friend, but they stopped when Longstint shouted, 'Don't follow, please! You will all be in danger. The quest is more important than one Willigrew!'

'He's right,' said Bronglay sadly. 'We must not follow.' In the distance he could hear his friend shouting and struggling with his attacker. Then everything went quiet.

Bronglay heaved a great sigh. 'We must go on now,' he said. 'Now we must succeed so that brave Longstint will not have died in vain.'

The four remaining Willigrews went on, tearfully, but more determined than ever.

As they made their way, more warily now, along the tunnels, they all noticed that the further they went the colder it became.

'Dear me,' said Dora. 'Is it my imagination, or is it getting colder?'

'Don't be silly, Dora,' said Krowfin. 'I'm cold too, and *your* imagination couldn't make *me* cold!'

As they spoke, a spiky, frozen little man came out from behind a rock. He was made entirely of ice and was wearing a t-shirt with 'I am Jack Frost' printed on it. He spoke in a cold, raspy voice.

'Hello, good evening and welcome. I'm Jack Frost and I'm hibernating for the summer, and you lot woke me up, so you'd just better be on your way or I'll be touching you and you'll be

FREEZING to death!'

'OOH ER MISSUS!' shouted Krowfin, rather rudely, as the Willigrews hurried past and rushed on down the tunnel. Jack Frost chased them, but they soon outpaced him. They did not look back.

The danger was not over yet, though, not by a long way. The next thing they knew, Krowfin, in his haste, had run straight into a web of sticky strands, which were strung across the tunnel. He was stuck fast (well, he was running).

'Help, help!' he shouted. 'I'm stuck fast!'

Bronglay and Zamborina tried to get him free, but the strands were too sticky.

Bronglay sensed serious danger and he was right: coming towards them along the tunnel was a creature that looked like a cross between a scorpion and a centipede.

Sticking out from its head were two enormous eyes. It had about 50 little legs, but, horror of horrors, at the end of its tail, which was arched above its back, was a huge sharp stinger, poised ready to strike at Krowfin.

There was nothing anyone could do to save him. The thing was now within striking distance. The Willigrews all groaned in terror.

Then, just as the poisonous sting started its deadly journey, a small furry shape burst from an opening in the tunnel wall, picked up a handful of dust and threw it straight into the monster's eyes.

'YARG!' it screamed, and started scuttling around blindly, banging its head against the walls.

'Quick!' said the rescuer. 'No time to lose!'

Bronglay, dragging Krowfin from the web, gave a yelp of surprise when he realised that their rescuer was not just a little furry creature, but a Willigrew, and not just any Willigrew, but Longstint!

They escaped through a hole in the web and

rushed down the tunnel, eventually taking shelter in a small cave.

'Longstint, you're alive!' squealed Dora, hugging her little friend. 'How did you escape?'

'I managed to wriggle free somehow,' he answered modestly.

'But you're injured,' Dora said, pointing out a cut on Longstint's arm.

'Just a flesh wound,' said Longstint, trying to look tough. 'I'll live.'

Zamborina dressed his wound (in a nice pair of blue trousers and a white shirt), and it was a much happier band that continued along the dark tunnel.

A little further along, the tunnel narrowed and everyone had to squeeze through sideways. Just as it widened again, the ground seemed to disappear suddenly, and with gasps and shouts the Willigrews found themselves hurtling downwards into the darkness. The glow-worms couldn't keep up.

The fall seemed to last forever as they rolled down a damp, slippery slope. Then, with five bumps, they reached the bottom. 'Ow! Ooh! Ouch! Ooch!'

'Everybody all right?' asked Bronglay, with

concern. They all said they were.

'Where are we?' enquired Krowfin, peering into the gloom. Just then the glow-worms caught up with them, and they saw that they had landed in a gigantic cave.

'Look,' said Dora, 'furniture!' And indeed there was furniture, arranged neatly throughout the cave. There were pictures on the walls and a log fire burning cheerfully.

'Do you think this is it?' whispered Zamborina. 'Heafod's cave, I mean.'

'I don't know,' said Longstint. 'It's very big.'

'Wait a minute!' said Dora excitedly. 'Can you smell chickweed custard? I can definitely smell chickweed custard.'

They were all sniffing the air and agreeing with Dora when a little brown mouse with very long whiskers came through a door pushing a trolley. He pushed the trolley up to a table and placed five bowls of custard on it, then five spoons and five mugs filled with chickweed tea. Then, turning to the Willigrews, he said, 'Heafod welcomes you and asks you to eat and drink, and he will be with you in a while.'

The Willigrews immediately sat down at the table and started to eat.

'Wicked,' mumbled Krowfin through a mouthful. 'This is delish.'

They had just finished when the mouse re-entered the cave. 'Heafod is coming,' he announced.

Through a different door – a much larger door – came what could only be described as a head on legs. Heafod's head was huge and must have been five or six times bigger than his body., which, although not very big was very muscular, probably due to his having to carry his huge head around.

He was covered from head to foot in short, light-brown (although he like to call it taupe) hair. His eyes were bright green and his nose was sort of purpley-pink, and he was a bit strange for someone who was supposed to know everything.

'Welcome to my home,' said Heafod in a soft, friendly voice.

'Thank you,' said Bronglay, bowing politely. 'We are honoured to meet you.'

'It is I who should be honoured,' said Heafod. 'Your tribe is one I admire very much, and you five have been very brave in making this dangerous journey.'

'You have heard of the Willigrews?' asked Bronglay hopefully.

'Why, of course, I have a special file in my brain marked *Willigrews A to Z*,' replied Heafod, 'but first you must tell me your names.'

After the introductions Bronglay asked Heafod their big question: 'What can you tell us about the very first Willigrew?'

All five Willigrews sat up very straight and waited for the reply.

Heafod began. 'Long, long ago, in the days before flared trousers, space hoppers and kipper ties, when winter ended promptly on 1 May, there lived a tribe called the Eirenicons. Now this tribe had super brains and, therefore, loved peace. One day, however, a disease spread through the tribe. The disease could not be cured and so, one by one, the Eirenicons died. When there were only a few left, they held a meeting to decide how to leave some of their wisdom and love of peace behind. After much discussion, they decided to try to create a new race of beings. So, in a casserole dish, they mixed the following ingredients:

    1 dove's feather
        (with the dove's permission)
    1 teaspoonful of white cloud
    2 seeds from the honesty plant
    1 teaspoonful of spirit of adventure

6 rose petals (pink)
1 gram of blue cloud
1 pinch of salt
1 drop of tincture of myrrh
2 drops of tincture of less
3 cups of self-raising flour
1 bag of cheese and onion crisps

'Then they mixed the ingredients together, and waited. Sadly, nothing happened and finally they all died and the Eirenicons were extinct.

'Many years passed in the dead tribe's village, but strangely enough the casserole dish remained unaffected by time, still with the ingredients inside. One day there was a great storm which destroyed all the houses and trees.

'One mighty bolt of lightning struck the dish. The mixture, charged with electricity, began to bubble. Then it overflowed, some spilling out onto the table. This went on for several hours, and then slowly, rising up from the dish, a green mist appeared.

'As the mist cleared, a little creature with a furry green body, big blue eyes and pretty pink lips appeared. It stood looking confused until its attention was drawn to another cloud of mist, which appeared next to it. After a while another creature appeared, smaller than the first, but looking just as beautiful.

'The little creatures looked at each other and

smiled shyly. The smaller one looked a bit frightened, so the bigger one put its arm round it, and they wandered off. The only food they could reach, being so small, was chickweed, which as you know the Willigrews love.

'One night, as they walked through the forest, the two little creatures were attacked by a wild animal and were rescued by tribesmen from the Willow tribe, so called because they lived in a willow tree. The two little travellers were well looked after by this tribe, who fed them, gave them shelter and taught them to speak.

'The two creatures settled with the Willow people and spent their days growing chickweed, which they needed to live. The Willow people called them "The Growers" because of this.

'The creatures, however, preferred to be called "Willow people", so they ended up being called "Willow Growers". This was a bit long, so eventually it became "Willowgrows" and, after a while, "Willigrews". The leader of the Willow people gave the two Willigrews names: the bigger one was to be called Bronglay (which meant "Leader"), and the smaller one was to be called Azurino because of her dazzling blue eyes.

'After many years among the Willow people,

Bronglay and Azurino had five children and were very happy. Something, however, was calling Bronglay. He knew that he had to leave and start his own tribe. So they left their safe home and went searching. After much travelling and many adventures, they found the perfect spot and called it "Willigrew".

'And that, my friends, is how your tribe started,' said Heafod, resting his huge head against the cave wall.

Bronglay and his friends sat in silence for a moment. Then Krowfin said, 'Well, I'll be blowed, what an amazing story.'

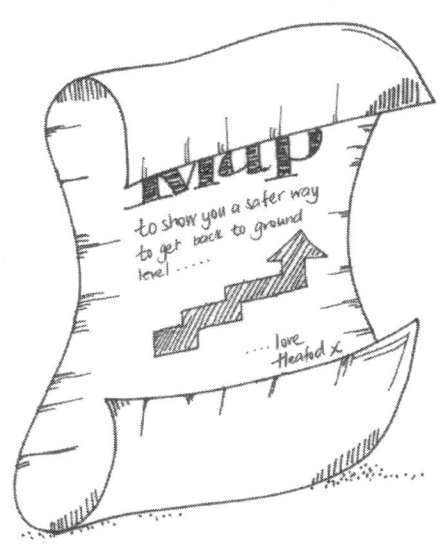

Map to show you a safer way to get back to ground level..... ....love Heafod x

The others agreed and Bronglay thanked Heafod, who asked the brown mouse to give them a map.

This map would show them a safer way to get back to ground level. They parted with much waving and went on their way back into the tunnels.

The journey to the surface was very steep, but much less dangerous, and in no time at all they were out in the open. They said goodbye to the glow-worms and started the long journey back to Willigrew.

All they talked about as they walked was Heafod's story. Dora Dingbat said that if she ever had a female baby she would call her Azurino. She looked at Longstint as she said it, and he smiled and wrinkled his nose. He looked better with a wrinkly nose.

It took many days before they reached home, but they eventually arrived to see a banner strung across the main street:

WELCOME HOME BRAVE WILLIGREWS!

A party was held in the Meeting Hall and Bronglay told Heafod's story to everyone.

When they heard about the dangerous journey the five Willigrews had undertaken, everyone praised Longstint for his great courage. The commander of the army promoted him on the spot. Then Longstint was asked to make a speech.

Wrinkling his nose in happiness, Longstint stood on a table to speak. He thanked everyone for such a wonderful party, with lovely food, especially the chickweed burgers. He then announced that he and Dora Dingbat had decided to become Willigrew and wife.

All the Willigrews cheered and hopped about backwards on one leg, flicking their earlobes.

84

THE WILLIGREWS AND THE GLOOPUDDS

This is the story about how the Willigrews came under attack from a band of really horrible creatures called the Gloopudds. The Gloopudds' leader was Graham the Grotesque, who was so ugly he couldn't wash his own face. All the Gloopudds looked pretty strange. In fact, the uglier they were, the more popular they were among the other Gloopudds, which is why Graham was their leader. Their motto was: 'Punching, kicking, biting, we are always fighting.' I don't know about you, but I think that's not a good motto.

As you may know, the Willigrews don't like fighting much and they avoid it where possible. The Gloopudds were the complete opposite. They lived to fight and loved attacking other villages and being very unfriendly in general.

This is how it all happened.

Bronglay and Yill were sitting outside their home enjoying a nice cup of chickweed tea and talking about this and that. Bronglay was talking about this and Yill was talking about that. As this wasn't very interesting, they decided to concentrate on that, and Yill said, 'What's that, in the distance?'

'That,' replied Bronglay, 'is a plume of smoke.'

Sure enough, in the distance beyond the trees was a long, skinny tower of white smoke spiralling into the sky.

'What do you think is happening?' asked Yill.

'I don't know, but it's happening outside Willigrew,' said Bronglay. 'If it's still smoking in a little minute I'll ask someone to go and take a look.'

Just then someone came dashing across the field. It was Krowfin, and he looked very agitated and confused (as usual). 'Fire, fire!' he exclaimed. 'The world is on fire! We're all going to die in our socks!'

'Calm down,' said Yill soothingly. 'You're not wearing socks.'

Krowfin looked down at his feet, smiled and said, 'Phew, that's a relief!'

Bronglay stood up and put his hand on Krowfin's shoulder. 'Don't worry, old friend,' he said reassuringly. 'We'll send a search party to find out where the smoke is coming from.'

'Oh, can I come?' asked Krowfin. 'I love parties.'

Yill explained to Krowfin that a search party was not a get-together with jelly and ice cream, but was more like a posse.

'I like cats as well!' said Krowfin.

Bronglay and Yill gave up trying to explain and started to make plans.

Bronglay wondered whom he should send, as it might be a dangerous mission. He would send Krowfin, of course. Krowfin was his left-hand man and always went on missions, whether he understood what was going on or not. Bronglay knew his faithful Longstint would not let him down, and his son Rewsin was very reliable. He would also send two of Longstint's best soldiers, Partive and Parsleno. The Willigrew army was not all that interested in fighting, but these two looked like they might be, at a pinch.

The chosen group gathered at the Meeting Hall and awaited their instructions from Bronglay.

'Right,' he began. 'This mission may or may not be dangerous, but I need you all to be very careful. The fire, in the distance, may be nothing to worry about, but I think we should take a look.'

'I have a question,' said Krowfin. 'Where is

the distance? I've never been there before. Who lives there?'

Everyone laughed and rolled about on the floor.

'Don't worry,' said Longstint. 'I know the way.'

Bronglay then said to Longstint, 'Don't, whatever you do, put anyone in danger. Just reconoit ... erm, reconter ... erm, recintor ... well, take a look and report back to me.'

The little band of Willigrews set off straight away and headed towards the distant smoke. They soon reached the edge of Willigrew, where a small crowd had gathered to wish them luck, carrying banners saying 'We wish you luck'.

They waved goodbye, and Longstint and his band marched off.

After a while, the Willigrews came to a clearing in the woods, but nothing happened there (I just thought I'd let you know). Nothing happened at the next clearing either, but when they got to the clearing after the next clearing, something did happen.

Oh! Of course, you want to know what it was.

Well, at first it looked like a crowd of feet standing in a circle, but when the group got closer they could see that it was a crowd of Feet standing in a circle. When the Feet saw the Willigrews approaching, they started to run around in circles saying, 'What's afoot?' and 'Upon my soul!' and 'My corns are playing me up!'

Longstint walked over to the nearest Foot and held out his hand in friendship. 'Hello, Foot, my name is Longstint and we are from the Willigrew tribe. We mean you no harm; we are going to see what the distant smoke is.'

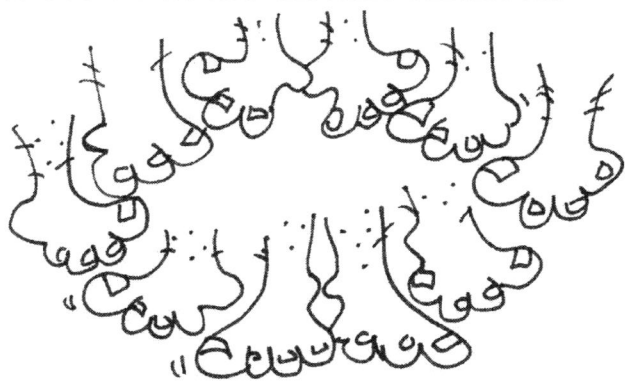

'That'll be the Gloopudds,' said the first Foot. 'You don't want to get involved with them, they're very nasty.'

Longstint was confused, as the Foot had no mouth but was speaking to him. He thought it would be rude to ask where its mouth was, however, so he didn't.

The first Foot continued, 'The Gloopudds are

all ugly, all spiteful and all have bad table manners. Be sure to steer clear of the one called Farter the Fragrant: he is one seriously smelly dude. Their leader is Graham the Grotesque, the ugliest thing you will ever see, unless you've seen something uglier, although I'm sure you haven't.'

The Willigrews all shuddered in alarm.

The first Foot went on, 'We Feet like to think the best of people, but in the case of the Gloopudds we can't. They just want to argue and fight all the time. They have destroyed every village in their path, so you have a choice. You can leave your village until they have gone, or you can stand and fight. If you fight, you will definitely lose!' He paused. 'Unless you win, of course, but you won't … well, you might … no, I'm sure you won't.'

There was a short silence. It was standing next to a tall silence, which everyone ignored.

'We must stop them from reaching Willigrew,' said Krowfin.

'How?' asked Rewsin.

'I think we should go and take a look,' Longstint replied.

'That would be very dangerous,' the second

Foot warned. 'We tried talking to them, but they threw their breakfast at us, eggs and bacon flying everywhere! We ran away before they started throwing the hash browns. Look, I've still got brown sauce on my big toe.'

Everyone looked at the second Foot, and they could all see that it definitely had a big toe and it really did have brown sauce on it.

Having seen this, the Willigrews knew the Feet could be trusted. Everyone knows that anyone who tells the truth about brown sauce is trustworthy. There is nothing worse than a 'brown sauce liar'.

The Willigrews waved goodbye to the Feet (the Feet waggled their toes in reply) and continued their journey towards the smoke.

The little band of Willigrews trudged on and left the Feet heading in the other direction. Their journey took them through a forest with very tall trees and very long grass. There was nothing short about this forest. The Willigrews walked in silence for a while, until Partive broke the silence (he was always breaking things).

'I wonder how far the distance is,' he asked.

'The distance is always a long way away,' replied Longstint. 'Even when we get there it will still be a long way away.'

Krowfin was feeling very confused and felt a headache coming on.

Eventually the band reached a sign which read:

WARNING!
GLOOPUDS AHEAD
DANGER!
LOW FLYING TOAST

The Willigrews could now smell the smoke from the fire, so they proceeded with caution.

Longstint went ahead of the others to take a look. He reached a clearing in the forest and, being careful not to be seen himself, he saw the Gloopudds for the first time. They were all sitting on the grass talking and laughing, and they were chanting, 'We chased the feet 'n' they all got beaten!'

There was one Gloopudd who sat alone, some

distance away from the rest. Longstint guessed that this was Farter the Fragrant, the whiffy one. A smelly haze surrounded the unfortunate Farter.

The next thing Longstint noticed was how ugly they all were. The ugliest of them all was sitting in the middle of the group. 'That must be Graham the Grotesque,' thought Longstint

Graham's face was frightening, with a huge mouth and horrible crooked yellow and black teeth. His nose was like a small hairy button and his eyes sat on the top of his head on stalks. As he laughed, his whole body, which was really just a big blob of fat, wobbled and rippled. If he had legs you couldn't see them, as they were hidden under the rolls of rippling fat.

Graham stood up to speak and all the others fell silent. He began, in gruff, rough voice: 'We will soon be arriving at another village, and I want you all to be prepared to be very nasty to everybody who lives there. The village is called Willigrew and the creatures that live there are very ugly indeed. They are a peace-loving lot, so we should soon overpower them and pillage their village!'

The rest of the Gloopudds leapt to their feet and began chanting, 'Pillage the village! Pillage the village!' Some even shouted, 'You Willigrews, we'll eat your shoes!'

I told you they were nasty.

Having heard all this, Longstint left to report back to the others. He told them what he had heard and that things were looking very dodgy.

'Many dangers lie ahead,' he warned. 'We must return to Willigrew and tell Bronglay about the Gloopudds. He'll know what to do.'

The others agreed and headed grimly back home.

As they walked, Parsleno, who did not normally say much, came up with an idea. 'I've come up with an idea,' he said. 'Why don't we send in a plant?'

'That's a good idea,' said Krowfin. 'I've got a lovely potted geranium on my mantelpiece at home.'

Longstint smiled patiently and said, 'I *think* Parsleno means we should send in a spy to find out more about the Gloopudds and their plans.'

They all agreed that this would be a very dangerous mission and that nobody should be ordered to go.

'I suggested it,' said Parsleno firmly. 'I should go.'

'Hold up a minute!' cried Partive. 'Parsleno will never fool the Gloopudds, he's not ugly enough.'

'Don't you mean not ugly at all?' said Parsleno, feeling a bit hurt. Partive apologised.

'Then we will have to make him look ugly with a disguise,' replied Longstint.

'First of all, we must cover up his green fur, or it will stand out like, well, like green fur,' suggested Krowfin. 'What about some wet mud?'

They all agreed that this was a good idea and started collecting wet mud from a nearby pond. They set about daubing the mud over Parsleno's body. The mud was a bit smelly, but it did the trick and not a bit of green fur could be seen.

The next problem was how to make Parsleno's face ugly. He couldn't stand the thought of mud on his face, so that was out of the question. They carried on searching until Partive found a fairly large leaf.

'We can make a mask from this fairly large leaf by cutting holes for his eyes,' he said enthusiastically.

After making the holes, Parsleno tried the mask on. It was an amazing transformation: his face now looked like a fairly large leaf with two holes cut out of it.

Just then Krowfin came out of the bushes with a dead toad in his hand and slapped it on

Parsleno's head. 'Finishing touch, or what!' he exclaimed. 'If that isn't a fashion statement, I don't know what is.'

They all agreed with Krowfin. So Parsleno, complete with dead toad, headed bravely back towards the Gloopudds' camp while the rest returned to Willigrew to see Bronglay and tell him about the plan.

Bronglay was not too happy about leaving Parsleno to face the Gloopudds alone, but agreed it was a good plan. 'Let's hope it works and he gets back safely,' he said. 'We must send someone to keep an eye on him, just in case he needs back-up. Any volunteers?'

Without hesitation Partive raised his hand.

'I'll go,' he said. 'Parsleno is my best mate. I'll leave right away.'

Bronglay agreed and started to make plans to defend the village against any attack by the Gloopudds.

Meanwhile, back at the Gloopudds' camp, Parsleno approached with caution. Caution decided to hide behind a tree, so after that Parsleno carried on alone. He walked bravely towards the fire where all the creatures were sitting.

'Hello,' he said, trying to sound confident. 'My name's Terence the Tetchy, and I'm here to apply for membership of the Gloopudds.'

The first to respond was one called Nosedrip the Nasty. He looked a bit like Graham, but had a really long nose that twisted and turned, and it was dripping, constantly. It didn't seem to worry him much, but it made Parsleno feel a bit queasy.

'My name is Nosedrip the Nasty,' said Nosedrip. 'I'm the Gloopudds' Human Resources Manager.'

Parsleno could see how he got his first name, but surprisingly, Nosedrip had quite a posh voice and seemed very polite for someone called

Nasty.

'Good morning, Terence,' Nosedrip went on. 'I'll get you an application form. Have you brought your curriculum vitae?'

Parsleno looked puzzled. 'Curlican what?' he asked.

'Your curriculum vitae,' repeated Nosedrip. 'Your résumé.'

'Oh, my razomee!' said Parsleno in fake realisation. 'You should have said. Sorry, I left both my coolican vito and my razomee at home.'

'Oh, that's all right,' said Nosedrip. 'I often forget things. Why, I once forgot to forget something and remembered it.'

Nosedrip handed Parsleno an application form, and he started to fill it in. The first question was easy: 'What is your name?' He entered his new name, 'Terence the Tetchy'.

The next question was a bit more difficult: 'What is your address?' Well, Parsleno's address was Foot of Ash Tree, Big Twig Sticking out of Window, Willigrew. He couldn't put that down! Parsleno had to think on his feet (although he was sitting down), and very cleverly he wrote 'Homeless wanderer'.

The third question was: 'Are you a nasty piece

of work?' He answered, 'Yes, I can get very tetchy.'

In answer to the next question, 'What are your parents' names?', he wrote, 'Mum and Dad'.

The last question was: 'Are you a team player?' Parsleno answered, 'Definitely, especially when I'm on my own.'

He signed his new name at the bottom of the form and handed it back to Nosedrip.

Nosedrip scanned the form, looked at Parsleno and said, 'That all seems in order. I have pleasure in offering you a position with the Gloopudds. Your main duties will be to be as tetchy as you can at all times.'

Next came the introductions. The rest of the Gloopudds were sitting in a circle (except for Farter the Fragrant). They eyed Parsleno with suspicion. The first to be introduced was the leader, Graham the Grotesque. He shook Parsleno's hand so vigorously that the little Willigrew thought his dead toad would fall off.

'Right, pay attention,' said Graham tersely. 'I will not repeat any of these names.'

He introduced Parsleno to Nunn the Wiser first, explaining that he was the brains of the outfit: 'He doesn't know a lot, but he knows twice as much as those who only know half as much as he does.' Nunn the Wiser had the normal 'blob of fat' body, but sported a selection of noses on his face. Parsleno thought it would be rude to count them, so he didn't.

Sitting next to Nunn the Wiser was a really small Gloopudd, and Graham introduced him as Nunn the Less. This little fellow was a very small copy of Nunn the Wiser, but without the noses. He just had the one.

The next was a really strange-looking creature whose name was Knigel the Knobbly. He had knobbles all over his face and body and on top of these knobbles were more knobbles.

'Knobbly or what?' Thought Parsleno.

Parsleno heard the next Gloopudd before he saw him. There was an almighty 'burp', so loud that the ground shook. He was introduced as Burp the Belcher. He burped again, though not so loudly this time. Parsleno waited for him to say 'pardon', but he didn't.

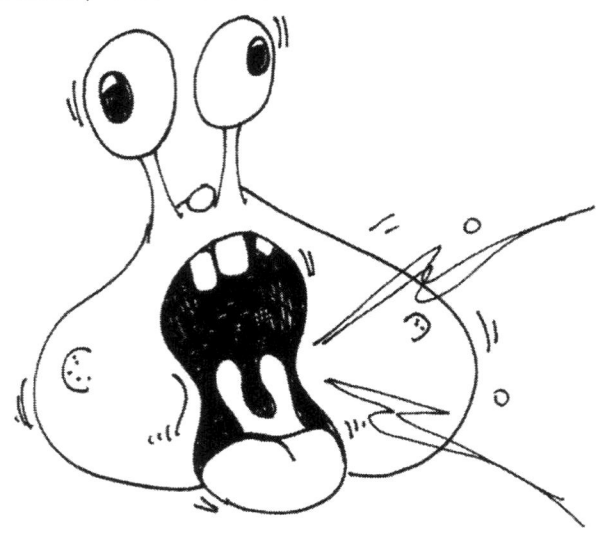

In appearance Burp had all the characteristics of the others, but had one large knobble on the top of his head. Parsleno wondered if he had caught it from Knigel, but didn't like to ask.

Victoria Sponge was next. To Parsleno she looked almost normal compared to the others.

Her skin was smooth, she had pretty eyes and a nice smile.

She too had knobbles, but these were matching and were on each side of her face. OK, so they had hair on them, but it had been permed recently, with lowlights. The other Gloopudds, however, considered her to be a bit ugly.

'I'm bored now,' complained Graham. 'You can get to know the rest later. Now tell us about yourself.'

'I'm Terence the Tetchy,' Parsleno began. 'I've been wandering around the forest for a very long time, looking for a tribe that doesn't think I'm ugly.'

'Ugly?' shouted Victoria. 'Ugly? I think you're very beautiful, and I just love the dead toad —

it's a nice touch, and so you.'

The other Gloopudds agreed and shouted, 'Hear, hear!' Burp joined in with a loud burp (again no 'pardon'), and Farter, well, he farted.

All the others quickly put pegs on their noses. These looked as if they had been individually designed for each different nose. Victoria, who was a bit of a fashion victim, wore a designer peg with diamanté-encrusted nostril blockers. Nobody offered Parsleno a peg because they didn't think he had a nose, as it was hidden beneath his fairly large leaf. So Parsleno had to put up with the terrible niff. It was so strong, he nearly passed out!

Knigel the Knobbly scratched one of his knobbles and said, 'Fancy a bit of grub, Terence? It's nearly dinner time.'

'I am a bit peckish,' Parsleno replied, wondering what sort of food Gloopudds ate.

'I hope you like lard, Terence,' Knigel enquired. 'We love it, and if we don't eat plenty of the fatty white stuff our bodies will shrivel up and waste away.'

Knigel handed Parsleno a plate, upon which was a large chunk of white, greasy lard.

'Get stuck in,' he urged. 'That'll put hairs on your knobbly bits.'

Parsleno picked up the lard and took a nibble. It was disgusting and made him feel sick, but he knew he had to pretend to like it. So he chomped away. The Gloopudds were suitably impressed and started to eat. This was a horrible sight and their table manners were awful (I did warn you!). They were slurping and smacking their lips, and bits of lard were flying everywhere. Even when it started to rain quite heavily, they carried on with their sickly munching.

Suddenly, to Parsleno's dismay, they all started pointing at his body. The rain had started to wash away his mud disguise.

'He's not a Gloopudd!' cried Graham. 'He's all green and furry, just like one of those Willigrews! And that looks like a fairly large leaf on his face! Get him!'

All the Gloopudds started growling and heading towards our little friend, who gulped in fear. Just then the dead toad came to life (it had just been asleep) and jumped from Parsleno's head straight into the crowd of angry Gloopudds.

What happened next was most unexpected. All the Gloopudds started to run around, trying to catch the unfortunate toad. 'Yummo! A delicious toad for supper, lemme at it!' shouted Nunn the Wiser. 'What a delicacy! A nice fat toad!'

Parsleno saw his chance to escape and started to run away. His flight was ignored at first, but just as he reached the edge of the forest someone shouted, 'You can hide, but you can't run ... we'll see you at first light tomorrow, and we'll destroy your village!'

Parsleno didn't look back, but just kept running as fast as his little furry legs would take him. Through the forest he went, dodging round trees, jumping over streams and occasionally hopping up and down on the spot in panic.

Exhausted, he stopped for a rest. Up ahead he could hear someone whistling a tune. He was a bit wary until he realised it was his friend Partive.

The two little Willigrews hugged each other and then did the Willigrew dance, hopping around backwards flicking their earlobes. They were so happy to see each other.

'What happened?' asked Partive.

'Well,' replied Parsleno excitedly, 'the disguise worked, then it didn't, it rained and washed the mud off, the dead toad wasn't, and jumped off, the Gloopudds noticed I was green, so I had it away on my toes, but not necessarily in that order!'

'Well I never did!' said Partive, although he wasn't really sure if he had done, but knew he might do one day.

Then the two little green fellows headed back to Willigrew to report to Bronglay. They found Bronglay and Yill waiting at the border. They looked very concerned, but were relieved to see their friends back safe and sound.

Bronglay had announced a meeting and had

invited every Willigrew to attend. The Meeting Hall was too small to hold everyone, so it was decided to have the meeting in the open air. A huge crowd gathered at the appointed time and Bronglay stood on a large stone and started his speech.

'My dear friends and fellow Willigrews, as you all know by now, Willigrew is under serious threat of attack from the nasty Gloopudds. Under normal circumstances I would arrange a meeting with their leader to negotiate peace, but these Gloopudds are not interested in that sort of thing. So we must prepare to defend our village.'

Bronglay paused while a murmur of alarm ran round the crowd. 'We all know that we will not be able to fight them off,' he continued, 'as we are not armed with offensive weapons. We must think of a way of outwitting them. Any ideas?'

There was general muttering from the audience. 'Hide under a bush,' one said. 'Run away or stand still and hope they don't notice us,' said another. 'Blow raspberries at them!' someone suggested.

The first to actually raise a hand was

Longstint; it was Zamborina's hand. Zamborina said, 'I think we should try frightening them off by making them *think* we're well armed. We could draw pictures of guns and tanks and hairy spiders and things and place them around the borders of Willigrew.'

This seemed to find favour with the other Willigrews and there was a ripple of applause, which ended in a crescendo of clapping and cheering.

Some even did the Willigrew dance by hopping around on one leg and flicking their earlobes.

Krowfin was next to speak. 'Right everyone, let's get organised. You three over there come over here and keep still, you six stay where you are until further notice, the rest of you move over to the bushes and then go back to where you were.' Then he said, 'Sorted!' and rubbed his hands together in satisfaction.

Bronglay smiled and thanked Krowfin for his suggestion, then said, 'I would like you all to split up into groups and each make a scary weapon to frighten off the Gloopudds.'

'Groups?' shouted Krowfin enthusiastically. 'Can my group be Westlife?' Everybody laughed and rolled about on the floor bumping into each other.

The Willigrews then split into little groups and set about drawing pictures of weapons they thought would be most scary.

They all had different ideas about which weapon to draw. Some decided to draw tanks, some drew pictures of fierce-looking warriors carrying bows and arrows, some drew big hairy spiders, one with its tongue sticking out. Krowfin drew an alarm clock. 'Well,' he said, 'my alarm clock always scares me when it goes off in the morning!'

When all the pictures were done, it was late evening. The Willigrews decided to stay up all night to await the Gloopudds' dawn attack. They all sat around chatting and singing songs. While they sat and spoke and sang, Partive sat alone looking thoughtful. Bronglay saw this and sat beside him.

'What's up, Partive, old green furry chap?' Bronglay asked.

'Well,' replied Partive, 'I was wondering why the Gloopudds are so ugly and we Willigrews are so beautiful?'

'I'll try to explain,' said Bronglay. 'I agree with you that Willigrews are beautiful, but only really to other Willigrews. I mean, a bristly old warthog thinks *he* is beautiful and if he saw us, he would probably think we were really ugly. The Gloopudds are beautiful to other Gloopudds because they love each other. If you really love someone, how can they possibly be ugly? After all, really beautiful creatures can do very ugly things and really ugly people can do beautiful things. I think it's important not to judge them on how they look, but rather on what they do.'

Partive thought for a moment and then nodded and said, 'Fair play.'

It was a long night for the Willigrews as they waited for the dawn. Some slept where they sat, and some, like Longstint, kept guard in case the Gloopudds decided to launch a night attack. All the drawings were in place around the border and everyone agreed they were very scary.

The drawings idea was, of course, Plan A, but Bronglay was worried that there was no Plan B. He knew that he had to have another plan in case the drawings did not work, but he just could not think of one – until a strange thing happened.

As Bronglay sat thinking, he heard a noise from a nearby bush. 'Psst,' it went. Then '*Pssst*!' a bit louder. At first he thought it was someone deflating a beach ball, but then he saw a small figure step out from behind the bush. He did not know it at the time, but this was Victoria Sponge, one of the Gloopudds that Parsleno had met.

'Hello,' she said, 'I'm Victoria Sponge of the Gloopudds.' (He knew now.)

She explained to Bronglay that she had made this dangerous visit to help the Willigrews. She was tired of attacking villages and wanted to settle down and become a fashion model.

'I'm fed up with getting my hair messed up in these attacks!' she said. 'In the last one I broke three fingernails and my perm came out in the battle.'

Bronglay was astonished to see a Gloopudd in Willigrew. 'I'm astonished to see a Gloopudd in Willigrew!' he exclaimed. (See, I told you so.) 'It's very kind of you,' he said, 'but how can you help us?'

'Well,' Victoria began, 'we Gloopudds have a weakness: we're not very fond of gherkins. In fact, they terrify us, and if you were to fire them at us when we attack, we would soon retreat.'

Bronglay's eyes lit up at this idea.

'I hope you appreciate my help,' said Victoria.

'Oh yes, that goes without saying,' replied Bronglay happily.

Victoria did not answer. She had gone without saying.

Bronglay hurried over to the rest of the Willigrews. He was grateful for Victoria's information, but wondered if this could really be a trick to catch the Willigrews off guard. Still, as he had not thought of any other plan, he decided to take a chance.

The Willigrews gathered round their leader and listened with interest.

Bronglay began, 'I've had a visit from a

Gloopudd, and she has given me some information that might help us save our village. The answer to our problem, apparently, is gherkins.'

'*Gherkins*?' everyone chorused. They all looked at each other blankly.

'Well, that's what she said!' Bronglay was now feeling a bit silly.

'Where will we get gherkins at this time of night?' asked Yill.

'I know,' Krowfin replied. 'There's a shop just a short walk away, called Gherkins Galore. It's open all night to catch the tourist trade. I'll go if you like.'

All agreed that Krowfin should go to the shop and get as many gherkins as he could.

When he arrived at Gherkins Galore, he noticed the owner standing behind the counter (he was wearing a t-shirt with 'I am the owner' printed on it, so Krowfin was a bit confused and wondered whether he was the owner of the shop or the owner of the t-shirt). He greeted Krowfin cheerily. Krowfin could not help but notice that this creature looked a bit like a gherkin himself. He was fairly skinny, fairly green, and if you met him in a jar you could quite easily mistake him for a large gherkin. He explained later to Krowfin that his tribe were called the Gherloms and were a cross between a gherkin and a lom (whatever that is).

'Good day, sir,' he said. 'How can I help you on this fine night?'

'I'd like to purchase some gherkins, please,' answered Krowfin.

'Well,' said the owner, 'you've come to the right place. What sort of gherkin would you like? We stock regular gherkins, organic gherkins, non-organic gherkins, gherkins we're not too sure about, gherkins we're absolutely certain about, cheese-and-onion-flavour gherkins, salt-and-vinegar-flavour gherkins, gherkin-flavour gherkins, pomegranate-and-pumpkin-flavour gherkins (very popular with my Gherlom tribe), short gherkins, long gherkins, thin gherkins, chubby gherkins, gherkins which have fallen on the floor and are covered in dirt and hairs, and, what's more, all our gherkins are pickled in the finest, erm, pickling stuff.'

Krowfin's eyes had crossed during this recital, and when the owner paused for breath, he just stared at him for a moment. Suddenly Krowfin jumped to attention. 'Wow! That's quite a choice.

I thought a gherkin was just a gherkin. Umm ... what would you advise?'

'Well,' replied the Gherlom, 'it depends what you want them for. If you want to eat them with fish, I'd go for the cheese-and-onion flavour, a perfect complement. Or perhaps, as you're a Willigrew, you would eat them with chickweed, in which case I'd go for the organic gherkins, which in my opinion are yummylicious.'

Krowfin looked a bit confused. 'I really wanted them to frighten off the Gloopudds,' he explained.

'Well,' said the owner, 'why didn't you say? You want our special "Anti-Gloopudd Gherkins"! They're a bit expensive, though. You see, they're farmed in the foothills of the Highandpointy Mountains, which are a long way away, so the transport costs are high and, of course, we have to think of our carbon footprint, don't we?'

Krowfin looked down at his feet. How did you make a carbon footprint? He pretended to understand, though, and ordered three dozen jars of the special gherkins.

The Gherlom lent Krowfin a small trolley in which to carry the gherkins home, and he waved goodbye and trundled off in the general direction of Willigrew. The trolley had two sticking wheels on one side and Krowfin walked around in circles for a while until he got the hang of it.

It was a dark and lonely journey home, but eventually Krowfin arrived back about an hour before dawn. All the Willigrews welcomed him back and gathered round to inspect the gherkins. 'Ooh look, gherkins,' said one. 'Yes, they're definitely gherkins,' said another. Parsleno said, 'I know a gherkin when I see one, and they're certainly gherkins.'

'Now,' said Bronglay, quite loudly, 'how are we going to fire them at the Gloopudds?'

Someone suggested throwing them really hard, but they all decided they couldn't throw them far enough. Someone else suggested firing them from a catapult, but they worked out that the gherkins were too large to fit in one.

'I know,' shouted Vectorn from the back of the crowd. (Remember her? She was the leader of the Skraks, and had been called Matcher before they discovered that the Skraks were really just grubby Willigrews. Now she and Bronglay took it in turns to be leader.) 'Let's make a dogapult.'

'What's a dogapult?' asked Yill.

'It's like a catapult, but much bigger,'

explained Vectorn.

So the Willigrew carpenters, Spokeshave & Nutspinner, set about the task of making the dogapult with gusto (and some tools, of course).

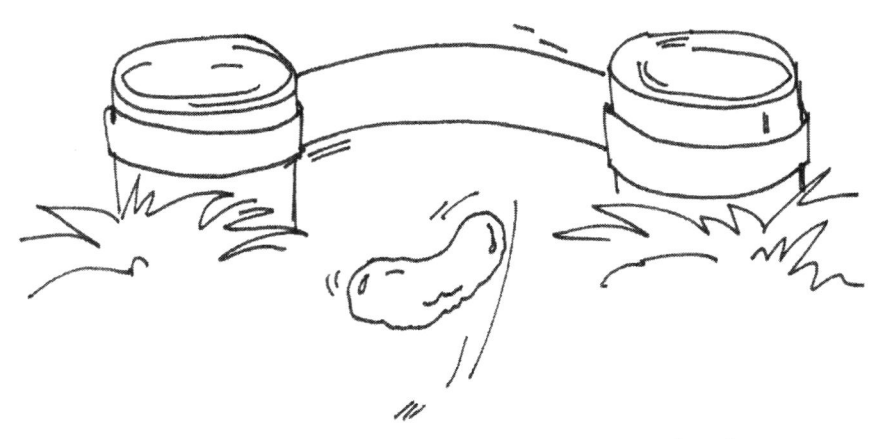

When they had finished everybody was impressed: it was made from two pieces of a tree trunk hammered into the ground with a large elastic band attached between them. It was decided that Longstint would take charge of the weapon because he was strong for a Willigrew. He appointed Partive and Parsleno to help him by loading the gherkins for him to fire.

It was almost dawn and the Willigrews could see the Gloopudds gathering on the hill to the north. There were about a hundred of them, and they looked ugly, even from a distance.

They stood threateningly in a long line and

linked arms. All except one, who stood some way away from the others, linking his own arms. The Willigrews guessed this lonely figure must be Farter the Fragrant.

'Listen carefully,' said Bronglay, so they all listened carefully and, sure enough, they could hear a distant drumming sound. The Gloopudds were stamping their feet. This sounded really scary and some of the Willigrews became very frightened indeed.

Bronglay walked to the front of his tribe, raised his hands in the air and said, 'Stay firm, brave Willigrews! I know you are afraid, but we must defend our village. I know you don't like fighting, but sometimes a Willigrew has to do what a Willigrew has to do. Remember we have the scary pictures and, if they don't work, we have the gherkins!'

'What if they don't work? Will they eat our ears?' asked a very nervous member of the crowd, who had a blanket over his head.

Bronglay stood straight and tall, looked down at the little blanket-covered creature, and said firmly, 'Don't ask, mate. I haven't got a Plan C. And don't worry about your ears – have you ever *tasted* a Willigrew's ear?'

As they stood and waited for the onslaught, Yill tried to calm them all by singing a little song, which went something like this:

Be calm, little Willigrews,
Be brave and strong.
The Gloopudds are coming,
And they won't be long.

They're ugly and nasty,
And smelly and rough,
And we know that Willigrews
Are not very tough.

But we have been clever,
So stand firm and still.
If the drawings don't stop them,
The gherkins will.

Don't let the noise frighten you,
Let me see no tears.
When this is all over,
We'll still have our ears.

Then, in the distance, a shout went up. 'CHARGE!' The Willigrews watched in horror as the Gloopudds gallumphed down the hill, led by Graham the Grotesque. They were gathering speed and would soon see the drawings. The Willigrews held their breath and waited.

As the attackers approached the drawings, they slowed down to a walk. Graham raised his hand and they all stopped. 'Wait,' he said. 'They look well armed. I didn't expect that.'

'We may as well go back then,' said Victoria Sponge.

The Willigrews heard this and hoped for the best. However, their hopes were shattered when one of the drawings started to fall over. It tilted quite slowly at first, but then fell faster and went crashing to the ground.

'*It's a trick*!' screamed Graham at the top of his voice (and he had a pretty tall voice). 'They're just drawings! Let's get 'em! They can't fool us with facsimiles!'

Bronglay saw this and stood at the front of his 'troops'. 'Steady the Willigrews!' he urged. 'Load up the gherkins and prepare to fire.'

Partive handed Longstint a gherkin in a flash. Longstint put the flash on the floor and loaded the gherkin into the dogapult.

'Ready ... aim ... FIRE! Let slip the gherkins of war!'

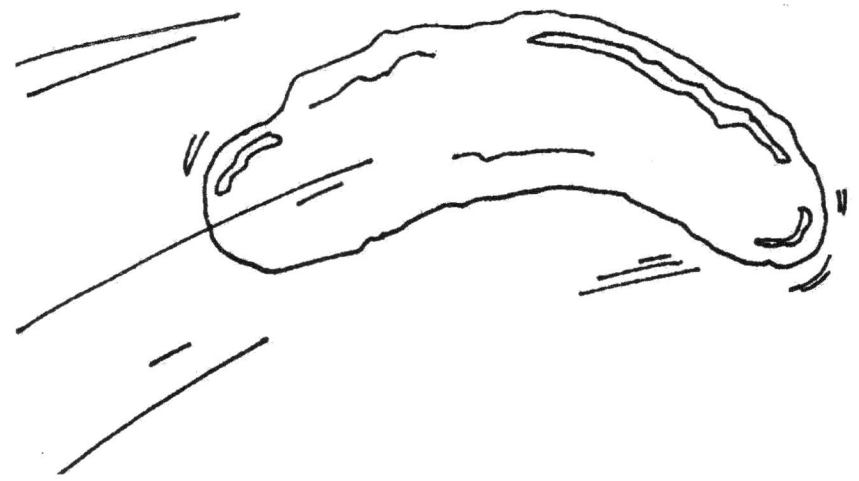

Longstint heaved the elastic band back, his little muscles bulging with the effort, and let the gherkin fly.

There was a whooshing sound as it travelled swiftly through the air above the heads of the crowd.

They all watched as it whizzed towards the enemy and crashed in amongst them.

'They've got a vegetable gun!' someone shouted. 'At least we'll have something to eat to celebrate our victory.'

The gherkin landed on the ground and the Gloopudds gathered round it.

'Hang on a minute ... that's not just a vegetable ... it's a *Cucumis anguria* ... a

GHERKIN!' yelled Nunn the Wiser.

As the knobbly green vegetable started to waft its vinegary smell upwards, the Gloopudds panicked. They started running about in circles shouting 'Run for your life! It's a gherkin!' and 'Arrrgh! We have a vegetable emergency!' and 'Flee the evil wallies!'

Longstint saw what was happening and started to load more gherkins into the dogapult.

'Fire at will,' ordered Bronglay.

'Which one's Will?' asked Krowfin.

Once he got used to the weapon, Longstint managed to fire more and more gherkins towards the enemy. They were now in a blind panic and the Willigrews cheered when they saw a crowd of them legging it back up the hill.

Farter the Fragrant was legging it on his own, as even in a blind panic the smell was too strong for the others.

The Willigrews all gathered around Bronglay and started to cheer and clap. Some of them hugged Longstint.

Everyone was so relieved that the Gloopudds had gone, especially as the solution had not involved violence, only gherkins. As you know, the Willigrews didn't do violence.

When things quietened down a little, everyone heard a small voice coming from beneath a small blanket, which was hiding behind a bush.

'Is it safe to come out yet?' said the blanket. 'Only it's getting a bit hot in here.'

Bronglay told the blanket that it was OK to come out, and then a head appeared with eyes blinking in the daylight. Everyone recognised Repscar, whose name meant 'Not the Bravest Willigrew'.

He had his hands clasped firmly over his ears. 'Have they gone?' he asked. 'Are my ears safe?'

None of the Willigrews laughed at Repscar, because they all understood that he was afraid and they all loved him anyway.

Then Yill said, 'This calls for a celebration!

Break out the Boogaloo chickweed and the chickweed champagne, and let's party!' She started the Willigrew national dance by hopping around on one leg and flicking her earlobes. Everyone joined in and danced around bumping into each other, which they really enjoyed. As far as our little green furry friends were concerned, bumping was the best.

As for the Gloopudds, I would like to say that they never returned to trouble the Willigrews again, so I will. They never returned to trouble the Willigrews again. There, I said it. I feel much better now.

THE WILLIGREWS AND THE BIG SNEEZE

You may remember that in a previous story (about the Time Case) I mentioned a Willigrew called Doc Dickory, who was named after his great-grandmother's favourite nursery rhyme. Actually, he was named after his great-grandmother's next-door neighbour's aunt's favourite nursery rhyme, but we won't worry about that. Well, he was the tribe's only doctor and he was, therefore, highly thought of by everyone.

Doc always wore his white doctor's coat and had a stethoscope hanging round his neck, even in bed. He hardly ever frowned and usually had a kindly, understanding smile on his face, which showed his rather large, sticky-out two front teeth to full effect.

Doc was a kindly soul who would never dream of taking advantage of his position. In fact, he was training an assistant to take his place when he retired. The assistant's name was Plister, which meant 'He Can Treat a Cold but Don't Go to Him for Dizzy Spells'.

One cold winter day, as Doc Dickory was saying goodbye to his last patient at his front door, he noticed someone running towards his surgery. It was Clarrynod Dillip, who was about 10 years old and lived just down the road.

She sprinted up to Doc's door, but the road was very icy, so when she stopped, she didn't, if you see what I mean. As she whizzed past Doc, she shouted, 'Please go to see my mum! She can't stop sneezing!' With that she disappeared down the hill at full speed.

Doc went back into his surgery and got his bag. 'I won't be long, Plister, I've got to make a visit,' he said to his assistant. He made his way carefully down to his patient's house. When he arrived, the front door was open, so he went straight in.

'Cooee! Mrs Dillip, are you there?' he called.

'Waaachoo!' came the reply. She was in bed. Doc sat on the edge of the bed and asked Mrs Dillip what the trouble was.

'Waaachoo!' she repeated.

'You've already told me that,' said Doc.

'But I, waachoo, aachoo, wachoo!' she continued.

'That's better,' said Doc, 'but it doesn't tell me what's wrong.'

Mrs Dillip started to look a bit angry.

'OK, OK,' chuckled Doc. 'I'm only joking, I realise that you have a bad foot. Oh, there I go again, kidding! I'll be serious now. When did the sneezing start?'

'Waaaachooychoochoo!'

Doc asked if it had started during the night. She shook her head and sneezed. He asked if it was this morning. She sneezed and shook her head. Then he asked if it was yesterday afternoon. She shook her sneeze and head.

'I know,' said Doc. 'Yesterday evening.'

Mrs Dillip nodded this time, but still sneezed.

'I'd like you to take these little pink pills. Take two every four hours ... or is it four every two hours? I tell you what: take half a pill every hour,' said Doc. 'If you're no better in the morning, I'll get my assistant to come and bless you when you sneeze.'

Doc said goodbye and Mrs Dillip replied, 'Waaachooeee!'

Doc was thinking about what to have for lunch as he walked home, but when he got there his waiting room was full to the brim with patients and, worse still, *sneezing* patients. In the corner stood Plister, looking very harassed, with a huge wad of cotton wool in each ear.

'Thank goodness you're back!' shouted Plister above the din. 'I tried giving them prescriptions with "bless you" written on them, but they wouldn't go.'

Doc Dickory was baffled and wondered what was causing this outbreak of sneezing. He found out by questioning the patients who could talk between sneezes that they had no other symptoms. They were simply sneezing.

'What I can't understand,' said Doc thoughtfully to Plister, 'is why all these Willigrews have caught it, and we haven't.'

'I see what you ... aaachoo ... mean,' replied Plister.

'Oh no, not you as well!' exclaimed Doc. 'I suppose it will be me next.'

Doc sent everyone home, telling them to keep warm until he found a cure. He then made some lunch and sat down to eat, still trying to think of a cure for this problem.

'I suppose,' he thought, 'this is an epidee ... I mean an expendim ... umm ... a dipinermic ... well, one of those things that everybody gets at the same time.'

Eventually Doc decided to take the problem to Bronglay, his leader. Bronglay was on holiday with his family, however, so Vectorn was in charge this week.

Doc went to her home and explained the problem. 'Sneezing, eh?' said Vectorn. 'Jolly old sneezing? A touch of the old achoos, eh?'

'Yes,' replied Doc. 'No other symptoms, no sore throat, no runny nose, no aches and pains, no ears turning green, just sneezing.'

'Well,' said Vectorn, as she chewed on a chickweed stalk, 'being a doctor, you should know that if you want to find a cure you'll have to find a cause.'

'That's easy for you to say,' remarked Doc.

Vectorn admitted that she did find it pretty easy to say.

The two decided that Doc should run some tests on the air and water in Willigrew to see what he could find out. He left after asking Vectorn to let him know if she thought of anything else that might help.

'Rest assured,' replied Vectorn. 'If I think of anything, you'll know before I do.'

Back at the surgery, Doc spent several hours running the tests without success. He then tried walking the tests, but still with no success. As one last effort he tried jumping the tests up and down on the spot, but that didn't work either.

Over the next few days the sneezing spread until almost everyone had to stay indoors on Doc's orders. As this meant that the Chickweed Beds were unattended, Vectorn became worried that the food supply would run out if the crops became overrun with weeds. She was pondering this problem when she heard the familiar sound of something coming through the letterbox.

'S'funny,' she thought. 'The post-Willigrew has already been.'

She picked up the letter, which had no stamp and nothing written on the envelope. She quickly opened the door, but the street was deserted.

Vectorn pretended to put on some spectacles. She did this because, although her eyesight was perfectly all right, she liked to practise putting specs on in case she ever did need them. This way, she thought, she would get used to them more quickly.

Inside the envelope was a small scrap of paper on which was written:

> *The answer is quite clear:*
> *If you want to cure the sneeze,*
> *You must go to the Seer,*
> *In the land of Antifreeze.*

Now Vectorn had heard about the Seer from her mother when she was young. He was an old, old man (he wasn't old twice, he was just very old) who had strange visions about the future. The stories about him all told how his cave was guarded by a fearsome pub landlady whose cry of 'Gedoutmepubyabard!' could burst a Willigrew's eardrums at 30 paces.

Vectorn shivered. Not in fear: it was just that someone had opened the back door and caused a draught.

It was Longstint. 'Hello old chap,' said Vectorn. 'You didn't make me jump just then.'

'OK, I won't apologise for making you jump, then,' replied Longstint.

Longstint explained to Vectorn that he had

spoken to Doc Dickory about the sneezing problem and wondered if he could help.

'Well,' said Vectorn, 'I've decided to go to see the Seer to see if he can help us. I've looked up the land of Antifreeze in my atlas, and it's a very long way away.'

Longstint volunteered immediately to go with her and promised to hand-pick four other non-sneezers to accompany them on what they knew would be a dangerous quest. They decided to meet outside the Meeting Hall on the following day at dawn and to make sure everyone wore their thermals because it would be very cold on the journey.

As most of the village was staying indoors because of the sneezing, there was no crowd to see the little group off. So they set off by themselves into a very cold, crisp morning, their feet making crunchy sounds in the snow which had fallen overnight.

In addition to Vectorn and Longstint, the others were Partive, Parsleno and Dora Dingbat (not much use, but, as before, good fun to have around). Zamborina had been intending to come, but she had started sneezing, so had to stay in the warm and eat hot chickweed soup and rolls.

Krowfin took Zamborina's place.

As the little green furry band got into their stride, they started to sing a little song.

> *We are crunching, we are crunching,*
> *In the morning, through the snow.*
> *We are crunching, all together,*
> *Walking slowly, in a row.*
>
> *Can you hear us, can you hear us,*
> *As we're crunching through the snow?*
> *You can hear us if you're near us,*
> *Walking slowly, in a row.*

They walked for most of the day without seeing anything interesting. Then, just as they were looking for a safe place to rest for the night, a figure appeared up ahead. It was a small creature bouncing along on one leg. You couldn't say it was hopping, because the one leg it had looked like all it was meant to have. Although the creature didn't look all that dangerous, the Willigrews hid behind a bush and listened.

As it approached, they could hear it singing, very loudly:

> *I'm a one legged Yaxi,*
> *And I'm looking for my home.*
> *I'd call for a taxi,*
> *But no one's invented the phone.*

Oh! I'm lost, lost, lost,
And I will be till I'm found.
I could find my way home,
If someone would lend me a pound...

Then it spoke the last line, rather more quietly:

I'll pay you back on Friday, I'm expecting a postal order.

Vectorn was first to come out of hiding.

'Goodness!' the creature said with a start. 'You gave me a fright!' It put the start and the fright in its pocket.

Longstint said, under his breath, 'We caught him on the hop...'

'Sorry, old chap,' said Vectorn. 'But you can't be too careful when you're travelling in a strange place. You could have been a robber.'

'I could have been,' replied the Yaxi. 'But I failed the entrance exam.'

He then introduced himself as Gonlee and explained that he came from a tribe called the Yaxis and he was lost because he had hopped down a rabbit hole and been forced to wait for the rabbit to come out and give him a push.

'What a shame,' said Vectorn. 'Where does

your tribe live? Perhaps we could help you find your way home?'

'Very kind, I'm sure,' said Gonlee. 'But you see, my tribe are travellers and only stop long enough to prepare to leave again. So I'll just have to keep on bouncing along until I find them.'

They parted, wishing each other luck, and the Willigrews decided to stop there for the night.

In the morning they ate some breakfast and set off again, wondering what the new day would bring.

After several hours of walking past trees and fields and hills and more trees and another hill and two toadstools and a very interesting broken twig, Krowfin thought he saw a Tyrannosaurus Rex carrying a handbag in a nearby field, but it was just a coat hanger that someone had thrown away.

Vectorn decided it was time for lunch.

Longstint put the kettle on and brewed some chickweed tea, and they discussed their next move.

Vectorn was first to speak. 'Well, my little band of green furry types, what shall we do next? Shall we carry on walking, or shall we just carry on walking?'

'I hate choices,' said Krowfin. 'They confuse me. Why don't we toss a leaf to decide?'

'Ooh! Ooh! Let me toss the leaf!' squealed Dora excitedly. 'I've got a GCSE in leaf-tossing!'

They all agreed that Dora was the most qualified, so she found a leaf and tossed it expertly into the air, saying, 'If it lands on its front, we'll carry on walking, and if it lands on its back, we'll just carry on walking.'

'Is that a choice?' Asked Krowfin, 'Sounds like half of one and six dozen of the other to me.'

The leaf floated slowly downabout in the cold morning air, twisting and turning and jiggling a bit on its journey. All the Willigrews followed the leaf's progress, watching it closely, moving their heads in a back and forth motion as it fell, until it eventually landed on the grass. It had landed on its back so its front was pointing upward.

'That's decided, then,' said Vectorn. 'Umm, I've forgotten the choices now!'

The others reminded her, and they agreed to just carry on walking.

On they went and, after passing the usual trees, fields and potential dinosaurs, they found themselves in a large clearing in the forest. To everyone's amazement, sitting at a desk in the centre of the clearing was a strange-looking scientist. The Willigrews knew this because there was a sign above his head saying:

PROFESSOR LONGWEDGE
STRANGE-LOOKING
SELF-EMPLOYED
SCIENTIST

As the group approached, Professor Longwedge looked up and said, 'Before you go any further, I need DNA samples from you all.'

'You need what?' asked Vectorn.

'DNA,' Krowfin interrupted. 'Deoxyribonucleic acid.' Krowfin knew a few things he didn't know he knew until he realised he knew them.

Professor Longwedge explained that everybody who passed through his clearing had to leave a DNA sample in case there was a crime committed and the authorities needed help with their enquiries. He then instructed everyone to stand in a queue in front of his desk.

The Willigrews lined up with Krowfin at the

head of the queue. 'Right,' said Prof Longwedge, 'if you could all open your mouths, I will take a swab from each of you.' Having said that, he proceeded to take a sample from inside their cheeks with a cotton bud.

Dora was a bit worried. 'If the Professor takes my swab now,' she whispered to Krowfin, 'what will I do if I need it another time?'

Krowfin reassured her that she had more swabs than she could possibly use in her lifetime and one less wouldn't make much difference.

The Professor thanked them all for their DNA and told them they could leave when they were ready. Well, I can tell you now that they were all ready, so they left.

Waving goodbye to Professor Longwedge, the little green band trudged off into the forest. 'He was a bit odd, wasn't he?' said Parsleno.

'Well, there was only one of him,' replied Dora. 'There are six of us, so we're not odd but even.'

They all laughed at Dora's words, except, that is, for Partive, who had climbed a tree to see what was up ahead.

'Can you see anything?' asked Krowfin.

'I don't know,' replied Partive. 'I'm not sure

what anything looks like. I can see *something*. It looks like an animal, and it's pretty big.'

'Erk!' squealed Dora. 'If it's a giant wasp wearing blue trousers and a tie-dyed halter-neck crop-top, I'm going home now!'

Vectorn disagreed with Dora. 'A wasp wouldn't be seen dead in that kind of get-up,' she argued, 'though you might expect it of a bee.'

'Did you know,' asked Krowfin, discovering that he knew something else, 'that really bees shouldn't be able to fly? Their wings are too small for their bodies.'

'Well, how do they fly then?' asked Parsleno.

Krowfin explained, 'It may be that nobody told the bee that it couldn't fly, or perhaps it's just stubborn. My favourite theory, though, is that they have a hidden solar panel in their furry bits.'

Then, from behind a nearby hedge, came a little voice: 'Did someone want fashion tips? My name is Trudey Jellegerk and I'm fashion editor for the *You'll Never Get Away With Wearing That With That* magazine. Available at all good newsagents, and one or two bad ones as well.'

All the Willigrews turned to look at Trudey as she emerged from behind the hedge. She was dressed in a trendy little number – the number 20, which really suited her.

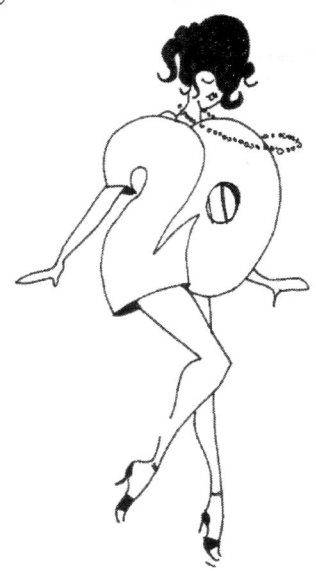

All the male Willigrews took special notice of Trudey, who was very beautiful. Krowfin just stared with his mouth open and his eyes popping out. His ears, however, didn't do anything very interesting.

Trudey approached the group and said, 'I love your green fur coats.'

'These aren't coats,' said Dora. 'These are part of us; we're born with green fur.'

'Well, I do beg your collective pardons!' exclaimed Trudey. 'I apologise to each and every one of you individually and all of you in a collectively together way.'

'That's all right,' said Vectorn reassuringly.

'Your fur is very beautiful,' Trudey continued, 'but have you ever thought of having some nice strawberry blonde highlights?'

'May I have some?' asked Parsleno excitedly. 'I love strawberries, especially with a big dollop of cream.'

'Yeah!' said Dora, hopping on the spot. 'Let's go and look for a strawberry shop which is conveniently located next door to a cream shop!' All the Willigrews started to jabber happily at the thought of strawberries and cream.

Trudey could see that her fashion tips were not needed in this situation, so she waved goodbye to the Willigrews and disappeared back behind the hedge.

Vectorn turned to Krowfin and told him to close his mouth and put his eyes back in. When he had sorted himself out, the little green band continued their journey, keeping an eye out for strawberry shops.

They had been walking for quite a long time now and felt that their journey must be nearing its end – and sure enough, soon after that a large mountain came into view. On top of the mountain was a gigantic sign that said:

WELCOME TO THE LAND OF ANTIFREEZE

There was a problem, though. Between the mountain and the Willigrews was a really huge lake, blocking the way.

Partive turned to the others and said, 'Wow, that's a really huge lake! How are we going to get to the other side?'

Longstint was, as usual, the first to volunteer. 'I'll swim across,' he suggested bravely.

Vectorn would not hear of it, saying that Longstint was very brave (she may have meant mad), but it was far too dangerous.

'What we need is a boat,' suggested Partive. 'But where are we going to find a boat in the middle of nowhere?'

'So this is the middle of nowhere,' said Dora. 'I've always wondered where that was.'

The others all laughed and sat down in a circle (they never went anywhere without one) and tried to think of a way of crossing the lake.

They sat in silence until, suddenly, someone singing disturbed them.

And the landlubbers lying down below,
below, below,
And the landlubbers lying down below...

The Willigrews turned to see a small boat coming across the lake. In the boat sat what could only be described as a 'small sailor'. He was dressed in full naval uniform.

His face was hidden behind a huge beard, which was snowy white.

His boat was called the *Salty Sandwich*, which was painted in red on a green background on the side of the boat.

'Avast there, me hearties!' cried the sailor. 'I'm Captain Cod's Eye. I'll be guessing that you may require some convenient nautical transport.'

Dora looked at the others and remarked, 'We don't want anything naughty! Bronglay wouldn't like that.'

Everyone laughed, including Captain Cod's Eye, who continued, 'Aha, scupper me main brace and splice the mizzen! I'll take you across to the other side, me beauties.'

Vectron thanked Captain Cod's Eye and the Willigrews climbed aboard the *Salty Sandwich*.

Once everyone was aboard, the Captain raised the anchor and started rowing towards the other bank.

He began to sing a song. He sang the first

verse, and the Willigrews made up the rest.

> *A life on the ocean wave,*
> *A home on the rolling deep,*
> *Where the scattered waters rave,*
> *And the winds their revels keep.*
>
> *A life on the ocean wave,*
> *A home on the rolling deep,*
> *Where the salty sea is wet,*
> *And you never see a sheep.*
>
> *A life on the ocean wave,*
> *A trip to the local shop,*
> *If you spill something on the floor,*
> *You can buy a bucket and mop.*
>
> *A life on the ocean wave,*
> *A cat will never say woof,*
> *A dog won't say meow,*
> *And something that rhymes with woof.*

Then everybody on the boat started to stamp their feet to the beat of the song and sang it all over again.

By the time they had finished, they were

nearly at the other side. With a few more pulls of the oars, Captain Cod's Eye announced their arrival. 'All ashore that's going ashore!' he shouted.

The Willigrews climbed onto the bank, thanked Captain Cod's Eye and decided to have a meeting. They didn't sit in a circle this time, because they had left it on the other bank as there wasn't room in the boat. Instead they stood in a row in front of Vectorn and awaited her instructions.

Vectorn began, 'According to my map the Seer's cave is over in that direction, but first we must decide how to avoid the pub landlady and her terrible screaming voice.'

The Willigrews scratched their heads. Dora scratched Partive's head.

'I know,' said Dora, 'let's confuse her with funny wigs.'

'How will that stop her from shouting?' asked Krowfin, quite sensibly for him.

Dora said she didn't know, but she had brought a funny wig with her and it would be a shame not to wear it.

'I think we need a diversion,' interrupted Longstint. 'Something to draw her attention away from us.'

The others agreed that this was a good idea, but wondered what would work on a pub landlady.

Longstint suggested that he should approach under cover of night and divert her attention by saying something that would make her leave her post for a while.

When the others asked him what he could say, he said, 'Umm … I'll think of something.'

Dora argued that saying 'I'll think of something' wouldn't work, and all the Willigrews laughed.

When it got dark, Longstint set off for the Seer's cave. The others wished him luck.

As he approached the cave, Longstint could see the pub landlady standing guard at the entrance.

She looked a bit fierce, short and stocky with permed blonde hair.

She stood with her arms folded and her big toes pointing upwards.

Longstint got as near as he could without being seen and then shouted in a loud voice (well, I suppose he wouldn't shout in a quiet voice), 'Landlady, we've run out of bitter and the barrel needs changing!'

To Longstint's delight, this had the desired effect. The landlady sprang into action. Her feet started running immediately, with her head following shortly afterwards. She disappeared into a neighbouring cave, rolling her sleeves up and looking determined.

Longstint turned and waved to the other Willigrews. Vectorn and Krowfin came over and the three of them entered the Seer's cave.

It seemed dark inside at first, but the cave

opened out into a large space which was lit with many candles. Our furry friends were a bit scared, but they need not have been. Sitting cross-legged on the cave floor was a little gnome-like creature with a face that was almost all smile.

'Hiya dudes!' he greeted them. 'How's it hanging?' Then he held his hand up and said, 'Give me five!'

Krowfin replied politely, 'Sorry, I've only got four.' He slapped the Seer's hand anyway, and everyone relaxed.

'So, what can I do for you today?' the Seer asked.

Vectorn explained about the sneezing problem and described the symptoms in detail.

'Mmm,' the Seer said. 'That's a toughie.'

He asked the Willigrews to give him a little time to think and told them to help themselves to tea and biscuits. 'There are some gypsy creams, some custard creams and some jammy dodgers.'

Everyone tucked in and much munching and slurping followed.

After what seemed like a long while, the Seer sat down in front of the Willigrews and said, 'I think that what you need is a bit of psychology.'

Before the Seer could continue, Krowfin explained in a worried voice that he couldn't ride a bike and would like to be excused that bit of the plan.

The Seer nodded wisely and continued, 'When you get back to your village, gather every single Willigrew together and ask them all, after a count of three, to sneeze. Repeat this treatment every day at the same time for five days.'

The Willigrews looked a bit baffled (except for Krowfin, who looked confused), but out of respect for the wise old Seer, they agreed to try his plan.

Giving them a bag of biscuits and a flask of tea for the return journey, the Seer said goodbye to the Willigrews and warned them to beware of the pub landlady who, he explained, was a bit lurksome and might be lurking outside.

Vectorn thanked the Seer on behalf of the whole Willigrew tribe, and the three stepped carefully out of the cave.

They were lucky. The pub landlady hadn't come back yet and they hurried away towards their companions, who had been waiting patiently for them. They all decided they should start back home as soon as possible, in case the pub landlady shouted after them.

When they reached the lake, Captain Cod's Eye was waiting to take them back across (they had booked return tickets).

However, they had not quite reached the centre of the lake when they heard a low rumbling sound coming from the direction of the Seer's cave. At first it was like a drone, but as it got louder the group heard a high-pitched scream.

'GEDOUTMEPUBYABARD!'

The words echoed from the mountains and across the lake towards the boat. When the sound reached the Willigrews, the boat started to rock as the landlady's scream stirred the water up into huge waves.

'Hold on, me hearties!' shouted Captain Cod's Eye above the noise. 'The sound won't hurt your ears – we're far enough away now!'

The others noticed that Partive had suddenly turned a strange colour, a sort of purpley grey. He leaned over the side of the boat and threw up. As the boat was lurching up and down, the puke was momentarily suspended in mid-air, then the wind caught it and it hit Dora smack in the face.

'Gross!' she squealed, as she wiped bits of custard cream from her face.

'Sorry,' said Partive. 'I couldn't help it. It's the waves. I never expected to see my lunch again ... oh look! There's a bit of jammy dodger as well!'

'You *disgusting* little Willigrew!' Dora complained loudly, although she half-smiled, seeing the funny side of the situation. The Willigrews never stayed angry for very long.

Eventually the boat reached the bank and the waves settled down to a ripple. One by one the Willigrews stepped onto solid ground, feeling very relieved. They thanked Captain Cod's Eye once again, and he rowed away across the lake.

Krowfin complained of having wobbly legs.

'Never mind,' said Dora. 'We all get wobbly leg moments now and again. You go through life thinking that everything is wonderful, and you wake up one morning and find you're in the middle of a wobbly leg moment.'

Krowfin patted Dora's head and said, 'Ah, bless your little furry feet!'

'Right,' said Vectorn. 'Let's get back to

Willigrew.'

On the way home the Willigrews talked excitedly about their adventure, but the journey back was pretty boring really. Apart from nearly getting trampled by a rampaging herd of giant whelks, almost getting squashed by a gigantic pilchard and running into a swarm of very angry flying Rice Krispies (there is nothing worse than angry breakfast cereal), nothing much happened.

Soon the little band of adventurers reached the village of Willigrew.

As they approached, a choir of sneezers greeted them. The whole tribe was there waiting for their return and looking very miserable.

Behind them was a huge pile of used tissues.

'Thank goodness you're back,' said Bronglay to Vectorn. 'Have you found a cure?'

'I hope so,' Vectorn replied.

Vectorn gathered all the tribe together in a row in front of her and asked for quiet. 'Right oh,' she said, 'I'm going to count to three and then I'd like you all to sneeze as loudly as possible. One ... two ... three!' she said loudly.

Vectorn held her breath (but it was a bit heavy, so she had to put it down). 'Come on now, a nice big hairy sneeze!'

But there was silence, not a single *achoo*. Suddenly Longstint, who started to sing, broke the silence.

If there's something strange in Willigrew,
Who you gonna call...
Sneezebusters!

Nobody sneezed. Everybody laughed and began to dance the Willigrew dance, hopping around on one leg, flicking their earlobes and bumping into each other as they joined in with Longstint's song.

THE WILLIGREWS AND THE HALF-BAKED SCONE

The Willigrews' next adventure started on a Wednesday. The day is not important, but I just thought I'd let you know that it didn't start on a Tuesday. Now, although many different tribes, most of whom were a bit dodgy and unfriendly, inhabited the country around Willigrew, the Willigrews' biggest friends were a tribe called the Dranglebinders. This other tribe were a bit like the Willigrews: they were peace-loving and didn't go in for bashing and biting and shouting insults.

The Dranglebinders were a bit taller than the Willigrews, and they were pink. Their skin was quite smooth and shiny and glinted in the sun. The Dranglebinders were famous for their glinting. They were quite skinny, but had large knee and elbow joints. Their faces were quite ordinary, with the correct number of features in the usual places, but their normal expression made them look very miserable. Not that they *were* miserable, they just looked it. Even smiling didn't help much.

The leader of the Dranglebinders was called Sirral. Sirral was a really nice bloke who would help anyone in trouble and had been good to the Willigrews over the years. The Willigrews had a saying: 'Sirral's all right, we owe him one.'

One day Yill was sitting in the kitchen drinking a nice cup of chickweed tea while Bronglay was arranging some chickweed flowers in a vase, when there was a knock at the door.

It was their old mate Sirral. He looked very worried and miserable.

'Come in, old friend,' said Bronglay cheerfully. 'How lovely to see you. To what do we owe this pleasure?'

Sirral slumped down at the kitchen table and

said, 'I'm very worried and miserable. I don't know how to tell you this, but I've lost my tribe!'

'*Lost your tribe?*' gasped Yill.

'Exactly,' said Sirral. 'Vanished, disappeared, gawn, and any other word you can think of that means not there anymore. In other words, they're not where I left them.'

Sirral explained that he had gone away for a few days to sit up a tree and think about ways of making his tribe even happier than they already were – and when he returned, they had gone. Not a single Dranglebinder to be seen!

Yill and Bronglay were as baffled as Sirral. The Dranglebinder tribe must have numbered a good 500. How could they all disappear at once? Bronglay asked Sirral if he wanted the Willigrews to go back to his village to search for the tribe. Sirral thought that this was a good idea and thanked his friend for helping.

'I'll get a search party together, and we'll leave straight away,' said Bronglay, trying to reassure the unfortunate Sirral.

Bronglay called for his son Rewsin and asked him to bring Krowfin, Partive, Parsleno, Longstint and Dora. He didn't ask Vectorn, because he couldn't leave his tribe without a leader.

When the group had gathered, Bronglay explained what had happened, and they set off to Sirral's village. As it was only two fields away, it didn't take the search party long to get there.

When they arrived, Longstint went ahead to make sure it was safe for the rest to go into the village. As it was all quiet, he beckoned to the others and they followed him down the narrow path that led to the first dwelling. There was hardly a sound as they entered the house. Everything inside looked normal, with no sign of a rushed exit, no sign of any struggle. When they checked the other houses, they were the same apart from a clock that was lying on the floor in one of the houses.

'I'm baffled,' said Bronglay, sitting on a bench on the village brown (well, it hadn't rained for several weeks). 'How could this have happened?'

Dora suggested that they might have found a last-minute holiday that was such good value that they couldn't pass it up, or they were standing in a long line one behind the other behind a tree, so they couldn't be seen from the front.

'Has anyone got any *sensible* suggestions?' asked Bronglay, patting Dora on the head and smiling.

'Well,' said Partive, 'I did notice one strange thing, but I don't know if it's important.'

The others asked him what he'd seen, and he explained that when he was in one of the houses he noticed that the oven door was open and, when he opened it, he found a half-baked scone.

Parsleno added, 'I did notice that the scoreboard on the village brown suggested that whatever game was being played was unfinished.'

'I think,' said Bronglay, 'that we ought to go back to the house with the scone and take another look.'

When they arrived at the house, Bronglay looked carefully at the open oven and at the scone.

'Look,' said Bronglay, 'look closely at the scone. Parts of it keep disappearing and reappearing!'

The others stared in amazement.

'That's really weird,' remarked Krowfin. 'But what does it mean?'

'I think we should take another look at the clock that we saw in that other house,' suggested Bronglay.

At the other house, Dora picked the clock up and gave it to Bronglay. He examined it carefully, and noticed that it had stopped and the minute hand was slightly bent.

'Do you know what I think?' asked Bronglay.

'What do you think?' asked Sirral. (Someone had to.)

'I think this is a Time Case,' explained Bronglay. 'And the whole of your tribe has been transported to a different time-space thingy.'

Bronglay asked the others to remember the time when Cringe had appeared out of nowhere. He had used a clock to travel, not across time, but to a parallel universe that occupied the same space as the Willigrews.

'Oh yes, I remember!' said Krowfin. 'You had to use your magic and say a rhyme to send Cringe back to Wimp. Do you think you can do it again with the Dranglebinders?'

'Well, I'll give it a good try,' replied Bronglay, 'but that was just one creature, little Cringe. I don't know if it will work with a whole tribe!'

Bronglay also warned everyone that a monster had come back the last time. It had been a friendly monster, but it had taken them ages to clear up the slimy mud from the lounge carpet.

Dora suggested that Bronglay use the same rhyme, but say it 500 times, once for every tribe member (typical Dora).

Bronglay shook his head and concentrated. Then he began his rhyme, which went exactly like this:

> *A whole tribe has gone,*
> *And this seems so wrong.*
> *So please bring back our neighbours,*
> *And return them to their labours,*
> *Or whatever else they were doing.*

The Willigrews and Sirral stood and waited to see if Bronglay's magic was going to work.

Several minutes went by (one minute was riding a bike and waving, another held up a sign saying 'Hello Mum'). Then suddenly, all at once and out of nowhere, came several loud bangs followed by several puffs of smoke. This went on for about five minutes, with more and more bangs and puffs.

Eventually the smoke started to clear and something very strange appeared on the village brown. There, to the amazement of all present, was a selection of legs, hundreds of them, all running around in circles and triangles and various other shapes.

'Oh no!' cried Bronglay. 'We've only brought back *part* of the Dranglebinders! We've left their tops behind!'

Before Bronglay could finish speaking, he was interrupted by several more bangs and puffs.

Out of the sky came a selection of DIY tools, hammers, screwdrivers and electric drills. There was also an invoice which Krowfin thought was pretty good value.

'Do you think,' asked Krowfin, 'that your magic rhyme has turned the Dranglebinders' top halves into a selection of very useful tools for general use around the home?'

'I hope not,' replied Bronglay with a worried look on his face. 'I'll have to think of a different rhyme and hope for the best.'

Bronglay concentrated his thoughts and tried again.

I'm going to try again,
To bring back the Dranglebinders,
But please don't send back tools
Like drills and angle grinders.

After several more minutes, there were the usual bangs and puffs, and then came the Dranglebinders' tops, hundreds of them. They whirled around above the legs and gradually landed with a *plonk* on top, creating whole Dranglebinder bodies.

Everyone clapped their hands in celebration ... until someone shouted, 'Hey! These aren't my legs, and they're too knobbly!'

Then someone else said, 'I've got the right legs, but they're facing the wrong way!'

'One of my arms is a screwdriver!' wailed another.

'Oh dear!' exclaimed Sirral, throwing his hands up in horror (he caught them on the way down). 'What are we going to do?'

'Don't panic,' said Bronglay reassuringly. 'At

least we've got them back. We'll just have to think of something else.'

Parsleno suggested that they had two options. Bronglay could try another rhyme, with the risk of something much worse happening, like a vicious bread roll with green ears, or they could leave things as they were and the Dranglebinders would have to try to get used to their new legs.

The one with knobbly legs said that he might be able to get used to them, and the one with the screwdriver arm said that it might come in handy. However, the one with legs the wrong way round was not so happy. 'How will I manage?' he complained. 'I won't know if I'm coming or going, and if I go somewhere I might be back before I leave, and when I get back I'll probably be half-way there!'

'Well,' said Sirral, 'I think you'll have to get used to walking backwards. We'll all help. After all, at least you'll be able to see where you're going.'

This seemed to reassure the unfortunate little Dranglebinder, and he wandered off backwards, falling over a little bit, then standing up and trying again.

When they were certain that everyone had come back from the parallel time, all the Dranglebinders gathered around the Willigrews, and Longstint shouted, 'Three cheers for Bronglay!' There followed much clapping and whooping and cheering and general happy silliness. (Or was it silly happiness? You decide.)

Then Sirral thanked Bronglay and the rest of the Willigrews for their help and both tribes did the Willigrew national dance, hopping around and flicking their earlobes and bumping into each other.

When things had settled down and the Dranglebinders had gone back to their homes, Sirral invited the Willigrews in for a bit of something to eat.

Sirral explained that he didn't have much in the larder, but he did have some instant chickweed porridge that he could rustle up.

'Yummeroonee!' said Dora. 'My favourite! May I have some honey on mine?'

'Of course,' replied Sirral. 'I also have some jangleberry jam.'

Sirral's wife, who was called Sirralsmissus, was sitting by the fire still recovering from her travels in time and space, but eventually she said, 'I hope I never have to go through that again, that was really hairy.'

Sirral asked her if she was ready to tell them about her strange journey, and she said she thought so.

'In your own time, of course,' said Dora, and everyone laughed.

As the others munched and slurped, Sirralsmissus began her story.

'I was sitting reading the *Daily Dranglebinder* at the table,' she said, pointing to the table where the Willigrews were eating. 'I started to feel a bit dizzy,' she continued. 'I got up to walk over to the sink to get a drink of water, when suddenly I was somewhere else! I knew it was somewhere else because it wasn't where I'd been when I felt dizzy.'

'What was it like there?' asked Partive.

'Believe me, this place I landed up in was seriously weird,' she replied. 'There were tools everywhere, hammers, spanners, pliers all over the place. I'd just started to explore when the rest of the tribe started appearing.

'We were all very frightened and didn't know what to do. Then we all jumped when a loud voice came from a small creature sitting on a workbench. It looked to me like it was made from wood shavings and glue.

"Choose the tools you want," the creature said, "and we'll deliver in a couple of days, but don't forget all prices exclude VAT.

Also, for one day and for one day only, we have a special offer on chisels, buy two, give one back. So the more you buy the more you can give back."

'We decided to humour the little wood-shaving creature and started to pretend to select some tools. Then someone shouted, "Erg! My legs have disappeared!"

'Within a few minutes everybody's legs were gone and we all hit the floor, *kerpludge*, together. I don't mind telling you that we were all in a panic by now. We couldn't run around, of course, so we all waved our arms about and shouted things like, "Where are our legs?" and "I'd put my foot down if I could!" Then there were two small puffs and a large flash, and we were back here with you.'

Everyone shook their heads in amazement.

Sirral thanked the Willigrews again for their help, and a little later, after much waving goodbye and blowing of kisses and general friendliness, the Willigrews wandered back to their village.

When they had completed the short journey and arrived in Willigrew, they were expecting a bit of a welcoming party. To their surprise and disappointment, they arrived to total silence. The village was deserted, not a Willigrew in sight.

'Oh no!' gasped Bronglay. 'The Willigrews have disappeared, just like the Dranglebinders!'

He need not have worried, however, because suddenly, from behind a bush, jumped Vectorn.

'Surprise, surprise!' she shouted. 'We're all still here, just thought we'd play a little joke!'

Then all the other Willigrews appeared and cheered the returning heroes. They all started to chant, 'Bronglay, Bronglay, Bronglay! You the man, you the man!'

Well, that's about it for this little adventure. We'll leave the Willigrews doing their national dance and let them get on with their lives ... until the next adventure, which will, of course, be very silly.

Dear Reader

I hope you have enjoyed these stories

Please visit our website

www.willigrews.co.uk

or follow us on

FACEBOOK or TWITTER

If you have enjoyed the book, would you be kind enough to put a Review on Amazon

Printed in Great Britain
by Amazon